DARE TO BELIEVE

BOOK ONE IN THE KAHUNA GROUP SERIES

L.A. SARTOR

QUOTE

Hope is not the closing of your eyes to the difficulty,
the risk or the failure.
It is a trust that if I fail now, I shall not fail forever;
and if I am hurt, I shall be healed.
It is a trust that life is good and life is powerful,
and the future is full of promise.

~ anonymous

For Mom and Dad, who always nurtured my "Lessie Do It" attitude. Mom, you always believed I could write. You gave me wings, and I'm flying. I love you. Dad, you're my hero, I wish you could see this, but then maybe you can, I believe you're always with me.
For my husband Gary, who never told me to give up on my dreams, who has the patience of a saint, and understands my need to hole up in my office and craft my stories. I love you.

1

THE MOVERS HAULED OUT THE LAST AND LARGEST PIECE OF THE furniture as Catherine Hemstead Malloy pushed the final suitcase into the rear of her old Subaru Outback, a remnant of her single days.

Scanning the small pile of boxes stacked near the moving truck, she decided it was time to get Haley and move on.

Cate had promised herself no looking back; onward was her new mantra. As soon as she drove out the imposing iron gates of the mansion her husband had named Highgate, she and her six-year-old daughter would begin their new life.

Tomorrow she started a society reporter's gig at the *Denver Post* and Haley started at day care. The mix-up over her interview at the *Los Angeles Star* newspaper ended all hope of getting a decent writing job, one that would actually pay her an almost living wage.

"Dude!" one of the movers cautioned.

Glancing over to the slate steps fronting Highgate's imposing doors, Cate saw Haley's armoire wobbling in the movers' grasp. The slighter of the duo struggled for balance on the lip of the chiseled stone step.

It took all her will power not to blurt out a "careful," knowing it would only earn her another complaint about the weight of the piece, and she was tired of their constant threats to escalate the price for moving the thing.

The heavy cherry wardrobe was Haley's choice of furniture to take with them to the new one-bedroom apartment. It held her toys, her clothes, and when she was younger, had been her favorite playhouse. It was the only furniture Haley wanted and, despite the ridiculously high cost of moving the thing, it was going to the minuscule apartment Cate had rented in Denver.

Watching as the two men navigated the remaining steps toward the decrepit truck parked near her ancient Subie, Cate appreciated the irony of the incongruous, even laughable, picture the vehicles made parked in front of the McMansion de Malloy. The huge pile of stone and plaster that had been the pride and joy of her late husband.

A new family was moving in soon, and Cate hoped this time the halls and rooms would be filled with laughter and love.

Fighting hard against the bitter memories worming into the already stressful day, Cate hurried around the perimeter of the house, aiming for the aspen grove where her daughter had begged to spend a last few minutes saying goodbye to her imaginary elfin friends. "Haley?"

Stepping into the empty clearing, Cate frowned at her daughter's disappearing act. "Haley? We've already gone through this. I promised we'd find another special garden in Denver. Your buds will come and play. I promise."

Nothing but silence answered her.

"Haley Marie Malloy, enough playing hide and seek! We're leaving. Now!"

Cate fought the tendril of remorse snaking through her soul. She rarely spoke to Haley in anything but calm tones. There hadn't really ever been the need to do otherwise, for her daughter, despite all the trauma she'd been through in the last six months, had never needed to be scolded. And if she needed five more minutes with her fairies and elfin friends, then, by God, Cate would give them to her.

Working hard to keep her pace slow, she walked the cedar path through the cool, dappled shade of the aspen grove, to the turquoise swimming pool and back again. Twice. Until her patience was burned through.

"Okay, baby, I'm sorry, but we really have to go." Moving deeper into the shady grove, sure Haley would jump out and try to scare her, Cate reached the high wall bordering the estate with no sign of her daughter.

About to retrace her steps back to the mansion, she stopped as a flash of pink caught her attention.

Hippity Hoppity Lippity Loppity, Haley's precious pink stuffed bunny, hung upside down on an aspen branch at the base of the wall.

Cate forgot to breathe.

It's okay, she's here somewhere. Just because Richard had died in a freak climbing accident six months ago didn't mean that something disastrous had happened to Haley. *Right. That's why you've been watching her like a hawk, because accidents* do *happen.* Even Luci, who sometimes babysat, was more alert now.

Pushing aside bushes, frantically checking the ground for any sign that her curious daughter might have tried to climb the wall and dropped Hippity, Cate saw only trampled leaves and a broken fern frond. The tree that snagged Hippity was too young, its branches too flimsy for even her rail-thin daughter to climb.

Cate grabbed Hippity, hugging the bunny tight. "Where's our girl, Hippity?"

A motor coughed and caught. The moving van! Maybe Haley had decided to play a trick on her mommy and hide in the armoire. The movers had certainly struggled with it.

The van was at the iron gates, ready to turn onto the county road as Cate rounded the corner of the mansion at a dead-on run. "Stop, wait! Stop!"

She sprinted down the long driveway, waving her arms. The wheezing of the ancient engine drowned her cries, and the van turned out of sight.

Cate backtracked and jumped into her car, throwing Hippity on the seat. The Subaru whined once, the ignition chattered, then silence. "Crap, crap, crap! Not now you pile of..." She wrenched the key again. This time nothing but silence, not even the telltale chatter of a dead battery. *If only she'd kept the Range Rover...* but thoughts like that were useless, there was no way she could keep up the expensive vehicle when it needed maintenance.

Reaching for her purse, she prayed the mover's phone number was on the manifest. "Thank you," she mumbled, shifting through gum wrappers, notes and lists for her cell phone.

It too was dead. Charging the battery had been the last thing on her mind. She threw the useless phone back into her bag.

Scrambling out of the car, Cate raced down the long winding driveway and onto the road. The truck was so far ahead.

Pushing her out-of-shape legs to pump faster, she ran down the center of the narrow road, frantically waving her arms. "Stop, dammit, stop."

∾

JASON ST. PIERRE PULLED SHARPLY INTO HIS DRIVEWAY AND skidded to a stop a mere inch from the wooden and iron gate as a woman running down the road, waving her arms, caught his eye.

Was that Cate? She was supposed to be gone by now, away from here.

Away from him.

He'd specifically stayed at his office in Denver to avoid any chance encounter, as the gates to her property and his faced each other on opposite sides of the county road. Drumming his fingers on the leather-wrapped steering wheel of the car, he couldn't believe all his careful planning was for naught.

He punched in the gate's security code, convincing himself to drive on. Then, unable to resist, he looked down the road again. Cate—blonde hair flying, long tanned legs pumping, arms waving like a flying monkey—was chasing something.

Let her go. Let it go. Let it be done finally.

But he knew it wouldn't be done, he couldn't be healed until she was out of sight, not for a day or two, or even a week, but for good.

"Damn." Jason backed out and within seconds pulled alongside her. "Cate?" he yelled.

Let it go.

"Cate, what are you doing?" he yelled again.

She pointed in front of her.

He looked. The road was clear.

She slowed and finally stopped, bending over, breathing hard. He stopped the car beside her.

"Why are you running down the middle of the road?"

"Haley. Van. Stop it," she said between gasps.

"What?"

"Moving van. Haley."

He didn't understand what she was saying, but obviously something was seriously wrong. "We'll catch it, get in."

The car's mighty horsepower made short work of the distance to the van. Jason laid on the horn with zero results. Waiting until they crested the hill and the road ahead was clear, he pulled even beside the van, only to hear the deep bass of hip hop blast from the windows.

Gunning the car, he pulled in front of them, turned the wheel hard and did a one-eighty.

The van squealed to a stop, running off the road onto the shoulder. "Dude, you crazy?" the driver yelled, swinging out from the cab, fists curled.

Jason met him before he took two steps. "We need you to open the back."

"Here? No way. Insurance."

"Please, my daughter may be playing a trick on me and hiding in the van," Cate said.

"There weren't no kids in the van when we locked it up."

"She'd be hiding in the armoire."

Silently, the men did as bid, then stood, arms crossed in annoyance, on either side of the ramp. Jason held out his hand, helping Cate up the steep metal incline.

He was stunned there was so little in the van. The house had been filled to the gills with furniture, art and knickknacks. Cate alone had enough clothes to fill this piece-of-junk van.

And why had she hired this company? Why not the best firm in Denver?

"Haley, you can come out, Mommy's not mad. I understand, baby."

Jason shot a glance at Cate, curious over the guilt lacing her voice.

They reached the armoire and Cate checked the left side, the open hanging area.

Empty. Absolutely empty, not even a hanger.

"I've got this side," he said. It was all drawers. He checked each one, knowing it was silly, but he had to make sure. He found a sketchpad in the bottom drawer and handed it to her.

Cate touched it softly, then tucked it in the gigantic leather satchel she carried.

"God, Jason, where is she? She'd never willingly leave Hippity behind."

"Let's get back to the house, check it carefully again, then if we can't find her—"

At her look of anguish, he amended his words. "Then we'll take it step by step. You can explain everything to me on the drive back."

She nodded, then swayed.

Grabbing her, he put his arm around her waist. Damn, she still fit perfectly against him. "Have you eaten today?"

"A banana."

He went down the ramp before her, holding her hand, just in case she had another dizzy spell. They headed toward the car.

"Hey, what about this junk?" the van driver asked.

"Take it—"

"Take it to the apartment." Cate interrupted, fished in her pocket for a second, then pulled out a set of old and worn keys, unclipped one and handed it to the mover. "Just put it all in there, lock the door, and give Barbara, the manager, the key."

"We need you to sign."

"Do it. She can sign later," Jason ordered, giving them an icy glare. It had them moving fast. They shoved in the ramps, locked the door and were on their way by the time he got Cate into his car.

"I'm really worried, Jason. What if she ran away?" Cate said and started chewing her nails.

Images of a little blonde girl with green eyes and a sunny smile flashed before him as he drove toward a house he'd never wanted to enter again.

～

JASON WAS GOOD TO HIS WORD. EVEN AS HE PAINSTAKINGLY searched through every cabinet and closet, nook and niche, Cate knew the house was empty. The connection she always felt around Haley was severed, a queasy emptiness in its place.

She followed slowly as he scanned inside the Thai-inspired pool house and through meticulously designed gardens—the Zen tea house in the Japanese garden, the playhouse cabin in the miniature forest, the calm aspen meadow.

Haley wasn't on the property.

Now, back at the front of the house, sitting on the topmost slate step in the shade of the stone portico, Cate fought full-on nausea. She had no one to turn to, no family, no friends. It hadn't mattered when she was single. All decisions she made affected her and only her. She'd learned the lesson of independence young and learned it well.

But Haley's disappearance wasn't something she could handle alone. And as much as she dreaded asking for help from the police, Jason, at her request, was now on the phone to Chief Anders.

Cate glanced at her former lover standing by his sleek red car, a deep furrow of concentration carved between his brows as he talked on his cell.

For an instant, the years fled, and she wasn't alone, the memory of him as he lay beside her, listening intently to her plans, with the same creases marring his brow. She'd reached up to smooth them away and he took her hand, kissed each finger ... then as quickly as the memory came, the solace of it fled.

Six years and a chasm of pain separated them, and frankly, she didn't have the foggiest idea why he'd bothered now to help her this much.

They weren't on speaking terms, civil only at functions where air kissing was the norm and you *darling*-ed your way through the party.

Jason never air kissed. He stood apart from that kind of phony cordiality. When she'd been on his arm, she'd admired his strength of avoiding pretenses. And when she was no longer a part of his life, she protected herself from the ache of his indifference by pretending he was an arrogant jerk.

The truth was Jason was a protector of those whom he thought needed protection and guidance. *Even if they didn't need or want his guidance.* These were traits Cate realized about him after the fact. And for most people these were admirable qualities, for how could anyone not want a protector, a defender, a guide? *Unless his way was the only way.*

She looked at him again, talking on the phone, making things happen, and bit her lip, knowing she wasn't being fair; he was helping because of Haley.

Jason's very strengths allowed him to be gentle and the champion of the innocent.

After Richard died, Jason hadn't minded when her daughter wanted to visit and play secretary with Luci, Jason's business assistant. Nor when Luci babysat. Or when Mark, Jason's live-in jack-of-all-trades, offered her a ride on the golf cart to the village store. And even when Marta, Jason's trusted confidante, allowed Haley to cook with her. They all got along great. *It's only you Jason doesn't want to be around.*

She walked over to her useless car. Grabbing Hippity off the seat, she held the bunny close. "Hippity? I wish you could tell me what happened to our girl."

She gently shook the bunny, then paused as a familiar scent wafted off the stuffed animal.

Sniffing harder, she shook the bunny again, trying to place the scent, but nothing would surface.

"Anders is meeting us at my place," Jason said.

Cate startled, so focused on placing the scent that it took her a second to realize what Jason meant. "Your place? I'm not leaving Highgate. What if Haley comes back? She'll be hungry and probably scared. I'm not leaving."

"You have no electricity, water or phone. Mark is coming over to be here—"

"Mark?"

"He volunteered. He's bringing an air mattress, a cooler of food, including Haley's favorite PBJ's, and several battery lanterns."

"Perfect. Have him bring two air mattresses. And Anders can meet me here."

They stood toe to toe. Jason's jaw worked. She needed to make him understand. "I know she was upset over the move, but I … we couldn't stay here any longer. I thought she understood."

"It's pretty hard for a six-year-old to understand anything like that."

Guilt ate deeper into her hearing him vocalize exactly what she knew in her heart. She could rationalize leaving the only home her daughter had ever known until the moon turned blue, but that didn't mean squat to Haley. This was home. This was where she played with her daddy. This was safe and loving, at least for Haley. She and Richard had made sure Haley knew they adored her... if not each other.

"Cate, the second she shows, Mark will call, and we'll be here in under a minute. But we need to get some food into you, or else you know what happens."

He held the car door open for her.

Her head did feel two sizes too big, and she had the shakes, yet she couldn't leave. "Mark can bring another sandwich," she said, knowing she was being stubborn, but not unreasonable. She needed to hold Haley the second she came back and it only made the nightmare worse to see Mark driving up in the golf cart, loaded with supplies. "I can't leave here. I can't abandon her."

"I'll keep the door open and a light burning so she'll know someone is here," Mark offered. "Hey, give me the bunny, it'll make her happy until you get here."

Still she couldn't take a step toward Jason's car.

"Compromise, Cate."

His words were a slap in the face. Compromise was exactly what she'd asked Jason to do six years ago. He hadn't heard her then... or maybe he had, since he threw the words back at her now. But he hadn't learned.

Slowly she handed the bunny to Mark.

Ignoring Jason's hand, she got into the car and it began to roll forward. "It'd help if you turned the car on."

His laughter rang out, rubbing her ire into high gear. "Cate, it's an electric car. No engine noise."

She felt his glance and turned to meet it, sobered by the worry she saw, mirroring her own.

He reached toward her cheek, then lowered his hand.

Relieved and saddened, Cate looked the other way as Jason accelerated through the gears.

Driving through the wrought iron gates of Highgate was a relief. The gates were as their name proclaimed: high, imposing and slightly gaudy, at least to Jason's eye. They were also a daily physical reminder of who lived behind them.

The short drive to his house was simply crossing the county road. And usually, when he drove through his gates, he entered his sanctuary.

The long drive lined with blue spruce and aspen ironed out the stresses of the day. Lush mountain ferns grew naturally, and lichen-covered boulders lay where they'd landed. Nothing was placed strategically by landscapers.

He had gardeners, just like the Malloys, but his crew, led by Mark, understood the land and the mountain he lived on. They worked *with* nature, not against it. The Malloy team transformed the grounds of Highgate into something completely artificial.

Today, with Cate beside him, the drive was not calming. He didn't want her in his house. He didn't want memories of them racing laps in his pool to haunt him—again. He didn't want her lemony and verbena perfume to linger anywhere—again.

But Haley was missing, and he'd do anything for the miniature of Cate. Haley should have been their child. And while he completely distrusted her mother, he'd cut off his arm before he'd risk harm coming to her daughter.

Chief Anders's siren split the air.

Jason had left the gates open, and the white Morrison Colorado Police cruiser pulled in right behind him in the broad circular drive fronting his home.

The front door opened, and Marta stood waiting in the deep, cool shade of the foyer. Marta was the only "family" he had. She'd been his aunt's right hand "man" and a financial whiz in her own right. She'd retired when his aunt died and stayed with him when not traveling. She'd been there through the "Cate" period. To Jason, Marta was his sixty-year-young ally, the only person he really trusted.

He followed Cate into the foyer, then glanced back at Anders, who looked around at everything quickly, as if making mental notes. Always the investigator.

"Marta, do you mind making us some coffee and sandwiches?" Jason asked.

She shook her head, then without any hesitation, hugged Cate. "Oh, honey, Mark told me about Haley. Don't worry, we'll find her. We all love our little Haley."

Jason kept his gaze glued to the floor as Cate dashed away sudden tears.

"We'll be in the office," he said, a bit more gruffly than intended.

Cate settled into the club chair she'd always preferred. Jason sat behind his teak desk, needing the barrier it provided. And Chief Anders paced until Marta brought a tray of sandwiches and two carafes of coffee.

She offered the platter first to Cate. "Okay, honey, now you eat. You have to keep strong, and you don't want any nasty ole migraine to get in the way," Marta chided.

To Jason's surprise, Cate did as Marta bade, even biting into the thick bread and chicken salad before Marta had offered the platter to the chief.

The chief refused.

Marta placed the platter on the desk and poured coffee for Cate and Jason.

Anders cleared his throat, looking at Cate. "Do you mind if we go through this while you eat?"

Cate shook her head, then put her sandwich down. Jason could have strangled the chief, making it sound trivial to eat at a time like this. But then the man didn't know Cate like he did.

Anders nodded to Jason. "St. Pierre filled me in, Mrs. Malloy. Said you've checked the grounds, the house and the moving van, correct?"

At Cate's short nod, he continued. "And apparently a special toy was left behind?"

Cate nodded again. "Hippity. A stuffed pink rabbit that goes everywhere with Haley."

"Has your daughter ever run away before?"

"Never!" Cate stood abruptly, spilling her coffee. She banged the cup on the table and stared at Anders. Her mouth worked, but she uttered nothing, and Jason watched as she took a breath, then another in an effort to calm herself. "But this move has been hard on her," she admitted.

"You didn't find any kind of note or Mommy letter or—"

"Damn! Haley's sketchpad." Cate smacked her forehead with the palm of her hand.

"I'll get it." Jason bolted from the room.

He was back in a flash with the sketchpad held between thumb and forefinger, and put it on the desk. "We found it in the armoire, bottom drawer."

Cate reached for the pad.

"Stop. Fingerprints." Anders used the sterling letter opener lying on the desk to turn back the cover. "Let me know if anything about the drawings looks peculiar or out of context in Haley's life." He flipped the pages after Cate studied each one.

Jason saw a family of three on the paper. Three blond heads atop stick figures having a picnic or playing in the playhouse. Richard, Cate and Haley. A few pages later, there were two blond heads. Haley and her mommy. She must have recently drawn that picture. Richard died only six months ago.

"Wait, go back a page."

Jason jerked back to the present as Anders obliged.

"This is odd."

"Why?" Anders asked.

"Haley's never drawn anybody but her daddy and me with her."

Jason saw it immediately. Haley was holding hands with a dark-haired woman. Beside them, Haley had drawn what looked to be a suitcase.

"Who does she know with dark hair?

2

"I CAN ONLY THINK OF TWO WOMEN. LUCI AND RICHARD'S MOTHER, Helene Malloy," Cate murmured, baffled by Haley's drawings.

"Luci?" Anders asked.

Cate was at a loss for a descriptor that fit Luci—Haley's playmate, babysitter? Once, Haley had wished for a sister that was as fun as Luci.

"Luci Roth. She babysits Haley when needed; she's my business assistant," Jason offered.

Had the circumstances been different, Cate would have been amused at Anders's confused expression. Everyone in Morrison knew about Cate and Jason and Richard, so the concept that Jason's staff would help the child of the woman who'd spurned him, then married his business partner, *was* confusing.

Even to her.

"When was the last time Ms. Roth babysat?"

"Friday," Cate replied. "For the entire day while I was in California for the *LA Star* interview."

"This Friday?" Jason asked.

"Yes. Luci was at the house before I left for the airport." Cate paused, remembering how anxious Haley was about her mommy leaving. Richard's death left deeper scars than Cate realized. She sucked in a breath and continued. "Luci left after I came home. She's very protective of Haley."

"And Helene Malloy? Does she visit often?" Anders asked.

Cate couldn't stop her snort of amusement. "Sorry. The Malloys live in Hawai'i . But even when they'd visit, Haley would avoid her grandmother. She was afraid of her."

"Afraid?"

Cate chose her words carefully. "Helene believed children should be seen and not heard. Haley's respectful, but she's curious and asks questions. That annoyed Helene and she snapped at Haley, and then at me for raising a child who didn't know when to be still. After that, Haley found reasons to stay away from her, and I ... encouraged it."

Cate glanced at Jason afraid she'd see disapproval of her parenting skills. Instead, the grin lifting his lips lifted hers.

"So, both are known to your daughter. Can you tell if either one of these women could be the one pictured?"

Cate scanned the picture again, looking for any detail, any clue. Both Luci and Helene had shoulder-length dark hair, and the clothes Haley had drawn were the simple A-line dresses kids drew on stick figures. The color, red, meant nothing; she couldn't recall if either woman wore a lot of red. The suitcase was a brown rectangle with a brown handle.

"Nothing about the women, and the only other odd thing is the brown luggage. Ours is green canvas."

Anders turned to Jason. "I'd like to speak with Ms. Roth."

"She'll be back tomorrow morning, took the weekend off."

"Then we'll talk to the Malloys. Do you have their number?" Anders asked of Cate.

"Yes, but I don't want them to know." Cate panicked, knowing the Malloys would be all over her, again inferring, perhaps now with justification, that she was a bad mother. Haley was their only grandchild, their only reminder of Richard. "They'll go ballistic."

"I need to know if they're on the mainland or in Hawai'i . There is no way they could have been here and gone back to Hawai'i since this afternoon. It takes them out of the picture if they're at home."

"I'll call them," Jason said.

"Speaker phone," Anders requested.

"You won't tell them?" Cate pleaded with Anders.

"I won't if I don't have to, but you have to let me do my job. Since there are two brunettes Haley apparently knows, we can't discount Mrs. Malloy, I mean the real, er, the other Mrs. Malloy, uh, I mean you are a Mrs. Malloy too—"

"I'm using Hemstead again. Not legally yet, but I'll get to it," Cate said as she pressed her fingers hard into her temples.

The headache that both Jason and Marta worried about bloomed around the edges of her eyes. Couldn't this have waited another few days? Why now, when she needed to be at her best?

Because this is the cherry on top of six months of stress. Six months of discovering nothing was as it seemed.

Jason punched a series of numbers into the phone as Cate closed her eyes and willed the migraine into oblivion.

"Malloy residence."

"Aloha. This is Jason St. Pierre. Is either Helene or Harve available?"

"Aloha, Mr. St. Pierre, this is Emme. I'm so sorry, but they're not here at the moment," the housekeeper's sing-song voice trilled over the lines.

"Where are they?" Cate whispered.

"Do you have a number where they can be reached?"

"They're at the ranch. The *ho'ohuli* should be finished by tomorrow. Mr. Malloy wanted to ride on this one, you understand? Can I have them call you when they return?"

"No, I'll call back. *Mahalo*, Emme." Jason disconnected the call.

"Of course, I should have remembered. It's the end of August and they'd be at their Big Island ranch for the cattle drive." Cate nodded carefully, mindful of her head. "I wasn't thinking of the date. Richard used to go every year at this time for the drive. He said his father was too old for the saddle, but I think Richard just got a kick out of being the cattle baron for a week or so. Harve will ride alone on this one."

Anders began pacing. "Since there is a suitcase in the drawing—is there any chance she would leave with someone on her own accord?"

"Haley knows the house rules. She could play in the aspen glen or the tea house, but Richard was strict. She couldn't go near the pool or the pond without one of us with her. I can't believe she'd wander off, let alone pack a suitcase and just leave, even with someone she knew. And furthermore, I didn't give anyone permission to take Haley anywhere, suitcase or not." The rant left Cate trembling from the migraine and an ice shard in her chest.

Anders pursed his lips, apparently impervious to her outburst. "I think she was coerced to leave." He held up a hand to stop Cate's interruption. "Listen, I can't do an Amber Alert on a runaway. You gave me what I needed when you said you didn't give permission. And there is a limited window of opportunity for an Amber Alert to be most effective."

Cate looked long at Jason, seeing nothing but support on his face, and at Anders, seeing compassion and determination. "Do it, then."

"I need a current picture, and though we don't have a suspect yet, I'd like to say Haley could be in the company of a brunette female. The CBI will issue the alert to all the media. And CDOT will post the alert on the highway VMS signs."

"VMS signs?"

"Variable message signs. Those huge digital signs on the highway to alert you to something."

Dear sweet God, her daughter was now the object of an Amber Alert. Cate moved by instinct to the chair where her satchel sat, trying to hide the fact that she saw only a kaleidoscope dancing in her eyes. She thought she'd reached inside the huge leather bag but grabbed nothing but air. She tried and missed again.

"Damn it, Cate, where are your pills?"

"Later. I can't take one now, it'll wipe me out."

"Where are they? You'll be better the sooner you take one."

"Picture first."

"I'll get the picture. Sit down."

Cate sank into the club chair and closed her eyes. She heard Jason rummage through her satchel. "The one in your wallet?"

"That's the most current."

"Good. This photo will copy well," Anders said. "The CBI will be involved the minute I make the call. Usually local law is the liaison between the victim's, ah, the missing child's family and the Bureau, so if you think of anything else, call me. We'll begin canvassing the neighborhood immediately. One more important thing. You have a cell phone, right?"

At Cate's slight nod, he continued. "And does Haley know the number?"

"Yes. Yes she does!" Cate opened her eyes and struggled to focus on the chief. "She could call me."

"Good, she might try. It's happened. Or with the assumption this is a kidnapping, there could be a ransom demand, so keep it turned on. The minute I hear anything, you'll know," he promised on his way out the door.

"Okay, Anders is gone, where are your pills?" Jason demanded.

"I can't ... charge cell phone ... need to be awake for Haley's call," she said, fighting the nausea that came with the headache.

"Don't be stubborn, just tell me where to look for the damned thing. You can trust me to keep the cell phone charged and at hand. And if Haley comes home, I'll take care of her."

And Cate knew he would. She didn't know why he was helping, but if he said he'd do something, he would. She clung to the momentary sense of safeness, of security, he offered. "The phone and charger are in my satchel, the pills are in the back of the Subie, inside my makeup case—it's black leather with a silver monogram."

Jason called Marta into the room. Cate heard them talk but didn't make the effort to understand them.

Thunder rumbled and a cool breeze blew through the French doors as a late afternoon thunderstorm rolled in. Cate shivered and closed her eyes again, giving in to the pain.

Moments later, she felt a soft warmness cover her. Blindly grabbing for Jason's hand, she caught it and brought it to her cheek in thanks.

Suddenly tears burned and flowed.

She cried for her daughter, not knowing where she was, what she was experiencing.

She cried for a marriage that had happened for the wrong reasons.

And she cried for a love that died so completely one night when it should have blossomed and flourished.

Dimly aware that Jason lifted her and cradled her on his lap, her tears flowed harder for the tenderness she so missed.

She heard Marta bustle in and obediently opened her mouth as requested, then swallowed when a glass was put to her lips. Still, she fought the pill's magic, knowing it would bring oblivion. Her body needed it, but she wanted to be awake to cuddle her daughter when she was found and returned to her.

Trust Jason to be there for Haley. She let that mantra play over and over, believing it to be true.

Cate's tears finally turned into deep sighs and within minutes, she was asleep in his arms.

JASON THUMBED OFF THE REMAINING TEAR TRACKS ON HER CHEEKS and brushed back the errant golden hairs tangled in her lashes.

This was killing him.

Haley's disappearance was gut-wrenching and holding Cate again after years of keeping his distance shredded his soul.

Lightning crackled around the house and thunder echoed off the surrounding peaks. Early darkness invaded the room. It all fit his mood perfectly.

He deliberated whether to let Cate sleep on his leather sofa or carry her to the pool house, but Marta made up his mind for him as she rang in on the intercom, telling him the pool house was ready.

Carefully rising, cradling her too-thin body in his arms, he pushed the French doors open wider with his foot and made his way around the pool to the small house complete with bedroom, bathroom and streamlined kitchenette built into the side of an enormous boulder.

The bed covers were already pulled back. Lowering Cate carefully onto the bed, he pulled up the soft wool blanket and left the light on in the bathroom, remembering her fear of total darkness.

He fought the urge to retreat to his sanctuary and pretend today had worked out as he'd planned ... with Cate gone, and he ... well, he would have been starting anew.

Instead, he paced the perimeter of the pool as the rain began to fall. Not a soft summer rain, but a deluge, drenching him. Still he paced, welcoming the seclusion the rain gave.

A shadow darting across the garden lights at the far edge of the patio gave him a start. "Who's there? Haley?"

Then a self-conscious laugh escaped his lips at his own foolishness. Animals were a part of living in the mountains. A deer, raccoon, or skunk had spooked him.

He slipped back into his study, pulled off his soaking shirt, plugged in Cate's phone, then poured a stiff brandy and stared moodily at the pool house over the rim of the crystal snifter.

Letting curiosity get the better of him, he rummaged again through Cate's enormous satchel to find the small leather journal he'd spied earlier when getting her phone out.

He started reading, impressed and saddened so much talent was wasted.

And he wondered how the *LA Star* interview date had been so badly screwed up. Dickerson, the editor, was on his annual two-week fishing trip. Cate was supposed to have gone to Los Angeles this coming Friday, not two days ago.

"Cate, wake up!"

Cate stirred, then was instantly awake. The headache was mercifully gone and Jason sounded excited. "Did you find her?" She looked down to see she was fully dressed, leapt from the bed, and flung open the door.

Jason, followed by Anders, stepped into the pool house.

She looked behind them for her daughter.

"Where's Haley?"

Jason shook his head and held up a wet and grimy pink backpack.

Haley's backpack. The one she had on when she left to say goodbye to her fairy friends at Highgate.

"It's her pack, but I don't understand. Where did you find it?"

"Under a bush near my pool. I was coming to check on you earlier when I saw a flash of pink. I called Anders when I realized what it was."

Cate held out her arms for the pack.

Jason glanced at Anders.

The Chief nodded and Jason handed it to her.

"Sorry it's a mess," Anders said. "The black is fingerprint powder, but unfortunately the pack was too wet to lift prints. We've been through the contents and found nothing more to give us any sense of who the brunette could be. I was hoping for a name or a phone number."

Nodding, Cate didn't try to hide the deep blow. She held only the pack and not her daughter.

Unzipping the pack, she lifted out Haley's pink ballet tutu nightie and ballerina slippers. She crushed the nightie to her face, inhaling the sweet scent, cherishing this tenuous link.

Stroking the slippers, she waited a few moments until she could speak without choking up. "So you're saying Haley was here and we missed her?"

"No, we think she was here while we were either at the van or Highgate looking for her."

"What? You mean she did run away? She came over and hid—"

"No," Anders said.

Cate looked at them blankly.

"Luci's not back," Jason said quietly. "She was supposed to be back at seven. It's nine. She's never late for a workday."

"Have you checked her suite?"

"We looked into the living room, it's oddly empty." Anders

answered. "I was about to further examine it, but Mr. St. Pierre asked me to wait, wanting you to be present."

Cate flashed Jason a grateful look.

He shrugged. "You might see something belonging to Haley that the chief would miss."

"I've called Detective Perkins in," Anders said. "He'll be here in a few minutes, but I want to get started."

Cate moved toward the door, ushering them out with her hand. "Then lead the way," she said to Jason, having no idea where Luci's room was located.

Luci hadn't worked for Jason when Cate was for all intents living with him. The residents of Jason's estate at that time were his aunt, who lived with him during her last months of her life, and Marta who'd moved in semi-permanently after his aunt had died. And if Cate remembered correctly, Mark had a small cottage somewhere on the grounds.

They reached Luci's suite, located at the far end of the house. Cate guessed it gave her some privacy if she was going to live and work in the same place. *And privacy if she were going to do something illegal, like take Haley.*

Anders pulled on gloves and opened the door. "Stay back, if I find anything, I'll bring it to you."

Cate nodded as she swiftly glanced over the living room. She wasn't sure what she expected, but not this sterile living area with only a leather couch, a couple of end tables and matching coffee table. A plasma TV dominated the wall opposite the couch. There were no knickknacks, no magazines or books, no pictures. It felt bare, unlived in... or recently vacated.

As Anders moved around the living room, something triggered a memory.

"There's something here." Cate took a step into the room, closed her eyes and let her mind go. She remembered instantly. "It's Luci's perfume! I smelled it on Hippity yesterday."

"You're sure?"

"Of course." She made a fast move for the bedroom.

Anders blocked her. "Stay back."

"I can prove it to you. But I've got to get Hippity back here."

She whirled around to Jason. "Can Mark bring back Hippity?"

In answer, he pulled out his cell phone about to punch in numbers.

"Hold it."

Jason's finger stilled. Cate spun back to the Chief in disbelief.

"That the scent is on the bunny isn't proof of anything. You said Luci was babysitting Haley last week." He put up his finger as Cate opened her mouth. "And by your own admission, she babysat for her many times before. Of course her scent would be on Haley's toy."

Cate slumped.

"Chief?" A wiry man in khakis and a polo shirt stood in the doorway.

"Detective Perkins, Catherine Malloy, mother of the child, and you met Jason St. Pierre last month at the county fundraiser."

Perkins nodded to them both, and Cate was pleasantly surprised when he reached out to shake her hand. She grasped it warmly, needing another lifeline.

He did the same with Jason and then put on gloves.

"We need a full sweep of the suite. We have Mr. St. Pierre's permission as warrant and I have probable cause, but be careful," Anders warned his detective.

"Can I stay?"

Anders looked at Perkins, who shrugged, and then back at Cate. "As long as you stay out of his way and don't touch anything. You're here only to observe. Got it?" the chief said.

She understood it felt wrong just standing around. Nevertheless, she nodded.

"St. Pierre, we have a few formalities over the warrant we need to finish," Anders said, and they moved off.

Cate watched Perkins move into the bedroom and followed, clasping her hands at her waist when he turned to check on her.

He swept the room in a grid, checking every drawer and under all the furniture. Facts he noted using the recorder hooked over his shoulder.

But there was nothing to check, nothing to ask her about, nothing for her to pin hopes on.

Then he opened the closet.

Cate saw a few ratty sweaters on hangers and the dark shadow up on the shelf, far in the corner. She moved farther into the room to get a better look, earning another glance from Perkins.

"Promise, no touching, I just want to see—oh!" Up on the shelf was a small brown suitcase. "Grab that bag. Haley had one like in it in her drawing."

She itched to take the suitcase out of his careful hands and rip it open. Instead, she had to wait as he again documented every move he made. Finally he unzipped the zippers and flipped back the top.

It was filled with clippings of houses and room designs.

Perkins laid them out on the bed. There were bedrooms, kitchens, pools, playrooms for kids.

Luci must have had plans for a new home, but then why didn't she take these with her? Cate wondered, beyond disappointed. "That's it, nothing in the pockets?"

He checked again, nothing. Then he turned back to the closet, taking down a large, fancy white box that had been hidden behind the suitcase.

With hands that looked too large to be gentle, he carefully slipped off the yellow velvet ribbon and opened the box.

Cate moved closer to take a peek, expecting a fancy negligee or designer clothes.

Nestled in layers of gold tissue paper was a miniature replica of Haley staring wide-eyed up at her.

A Just-Like-Me doll.

The scream started in her chest and burst through her lips. "Jason, come back."

She ran to the door and yelled again.

Jason and Anders came running.

With a shaking finger she pointed to the box.

Jason moved to take a closer look. "That's freaky."

"Those dolls cost hundreds and hundreds of dollars. They only make a few thousand of them a year. How could Luci afford one? Why would she have one made of Haley?"

"A gift? You did say she babysat often," Anders asked as he and Detective Perkins placed the doll on the bed and carefully removed each layer of tissue to check for a card or receipt.

Cate couldn't stand looking at it another minute and moved to the French doors. "I can't imagine giving this kind of expensive doll as a gift to a neighbor's child."

She glanced out the glass doors, noting the sun shone with the brightness that followed a storm-scoured night. How could it be so perfect outside when she was going through such horror?

And Haley? Cate couldn't think about what Haley might be going through, or she'd go mad.

BACK IN JASON'S SANCTUARY, CATE PACED THE ROOM AS HE MADE A copy of Luci's file for Anders. It was driving her crazy to simply sit. She needed to be out, doing something. *What? You have to let the professionals do their job. You asked for them, remember?*

Yes, she remembered, yet she was sure neither Jason nor Anders really believed Luci could take another woman's child.

"Here you are," Mark said, standing at the door.

"Come on in," Jason invited.

Mark came in, but stayed near the door. "I was getting breakfast and coffee to take back to Highgate, when Marta told me about Luci. You really think she could do this? Take Haley?"

"Her behavior leads me to believe she's guilty. Did Marta tell you about the Just-Like-Me doll?" Cate asked.

"Yeah, very strange." He turned to Jason. "My flight leaves tonight for the competition, but I'll be happy to stick around if I can help in any way."

"Damn, I totally forgot about the competition." Jason turned to Cate. "Think it's okay if he leaves his post at Highgate?"

"Yes, of course." She looked at Mark sheepishly. "I forgot you were still there—finding the pack and all the rest knocked it out of my mind. Thank you for being so kind and looking out for both me and Haley."

Cate gave him a peck on the cheek.

"Well, then, I guess I'll go check my gear and pack," he said and left the room.

"Not the most socially adept man, but a great estate manager," Jason said, then got up from his desk and handed her a sheaf of papers.

She scanned the top page, realizing Jason had given her Luci's background check. "This is what you copied for Anders, and you're okay with me reading it?"

"Why should Anders know something you don't?"

She began to read. It was impressive. Luci had a Master's in finance from the University of Colorado. She was the econ department's Omicron Delta Epsilon honor society member her senior year, and the youngest citizen slalom champion in Steamboat, but she didn't carry on with the sport after a nasty concussion. About six years ago her father had filed for bankruptcy just before a fatal heart attack.

Luci had absolutely no legal blemishes anywhere except for a parking ticket back when she was a frosh. Jason was thorough in vetting his employees, and this kind of detail wouldn't come cheap.

Anders barged into the room still talking on his cell phone. "Thanks, got it." He ended the call. "The doll company says it was a phone order. They didn't want to tell me much until I explained it was a possible abduction case, but eventually they did say Ms. Roth ordered the doll and it was sent here. And they're concerned, asked that we keep a lid on this," Anders reported. "Unfortunately, we've heard nothing from the neighborhood canvas or the Amber Alert."

Jason handed him a copy of Luci's file.

"Luci's mom still lives in Steamboat," Cate said before he could open the folder. "What if Luci went there to hide?"

"Why would she?" Anders asked as he turned the pages of the report.

"Why would she take Haley to begin with?"

"We can't be sure it was Ms. Roth."

Cate turned and pinned Anders with a defiant stare. "I'm sure," and crossed her arms, waiting for the chief to finish reading the information.

"She was pretty much a loner," Anders commented as he closed the file. "Her list of references and friends was pretty short." He was silent for a few moments. "I've got a buddy in the department up there who owes a favor or two. Let me see what I can do to get someone to check on the house."

And he left the room.

"If he can't persuade anybody to check, can we go up? I can't just sit here, Jason, it's killing me to do nothing. It would take, what? Three hours to get there in your fancy car?"

"Tops."

Jason knew this was coming. He'd known Cate so well once, and knew she'd eventually kick into gear and want to kick ass. She had the instincts of a bull terrier when she got an idea, be it for an op-ed piece ... or anything else. "Let's give the chief's connection a chance."

Cate paced from one end of his office to the other, then sat down only to spring back up and start pacing again, reminding Jason of his old Jack-In-The-Box toy.

Finally, Anders came back into the office, a grim smile on his face. "Luck is with us today. My buddy had a deputy in the area who knew exactly where the Roth house was located." Anders looked at his notes. "Which is not in Steamboat, but in the county. Sergeant Smith knocked on the door, and when nobody answered, looked around the outside of the house and in through the windows, just to be sure nobody was hiding. Apparently, whoever was there left in a hurry. The TV was set on a cartoon channel, a milk carton was on the table along with a box of Honey Nut Cheerios and—"

"That's Haley's favorite breakfast."

"Anyway, with the alert out and the apparent abrupt vacating of the house, they're asking for a warrant."

"Then we can go up," Cate said to Jason. "I don't think Haley's going to *just* come home, and I'd like to see firsthand whatever else they find there."

"Any problem with that, Chief?" Jason asked.

"Not any problem you haven't already heard. Don't make me regret this."

"Right," Jason agreed as the chief left. He turned to Cate. "What do you need from your car?"

"Nothing, all my clothes are at the apartment. But Jace, we need to get Hippity, just in case."

Jason worked the intercom, and by the time they left the house to get in the car, the stuffed bunny was already waiting for them.

Cate had wanted to thank Mark again, but he was nowhere to be seen.

3
_____

THE DRIVE UP I-70 WITH THE TOP DOWN ON THE CAR COULD HAVE been perfect.

The sun was shining hot in the Rockies, the sky crystal clear from the storm last night, and the piney scent from the lodgepoles and blue spruce blanketing the mountains rounded out the flawless day.

Except that Jason was still smarting from his reaction to Cate's slip of using the nickname she'd always called him.

Jace.

It had caused too much instant bruising to let happen again. He had to maintain some measure of distance to keep sane. In fact, he was insane to think he could be around her at all.

He'd learned the art of self-preservation in a long and painful journey, and being around her now, even for as vital a cause as finding Haley, would test his resolve to maintain a healthy emotional distance from the past.

Then maybe you shouldn't have chased her down yesterday and gotten involved.

"Jason!" Cate pointed to the huge VMS sign over the highway broadcasting Haley's Amber Alert.

Jason braked hard, earning an irate horn blast from the driver behind him, and swerved to the shoulder.

Enormous digital letters told the world that Haley Malloy was an abducted child.

Cate got out and stood staring at the sign, hands fisted on her hips.

Then, to his utter amazement, she raised her fist at the sign and yelled, "Bitch."

She stomped back to the car. "God, I can't wait to get my hands on Luci. What in the hell was she thinking, taking my child? For what reason?"

Cate grabbed his arm as he was about to pull out onto the highway.

He screeched to a halt again. "What?"

"Did she ever want children? Was she having a relationship?"

"I don't know. Her private life was hers."

Cate flopped back in her seat, arms crossed, obviously unwilling for his answer to be the end of that train of thought.

"There has to be a reason. I want her to tell me to my face."

"If she did this, then me too." Jason pulled out behind a convoy of semis crawling up the steep grade nearing the Eisenhower Tunnel.

"*If* she did this?"

"I know you believe with all your heart she did, but I need more proof."

"How much more proof do you want? How sure are you? Fifty percent, ninety percent? I'm at one hundred percent."

"I'm here, aren't I?"

Irritated by the snail's pace of the trucks and Cate's questioning his commitment, he maneuvered into the left lane, let the powerful car do its thing, and flew past the long series of trucks, only slowing when they entered the frigid, damp tunnel dug beneath the monolithic peaks of the Continental Divide.

He wasn't a fan of the tunnel, trying not to think of how much tonnage sat above him, and the convertible made the short drive more eerie than usual.

Cate, who usually fidgeted nervously in the tunnel, sat as still as the rock high above them. He glanced at her once and knew from past experience she was working out the problem of Luci in her head.

And since there wasn't much to go on, it must be driving her crazy.

Back in the sun on the other side of the mountain, Jason let the car coast down the steep grade toward Silverthorne.

"That's better," Cate said, relief evident in her voice. "Jason, I'm sorry I lashed out at you. You've been ... unbelievably wonderful and I've been, well—"

"You've been under a huge amount of stress. Let it go. I'm fine." He didn't want her gratitude, that would only make a dent in his armor.

He negotiated the steep turns, grateful they kept him occupied because her stare could have burned holes in him.

"I have a question."

"Fire away."

"What competition was Mark talking about?"

Jason laughed and felt some of the tension of the past hour flee. That wasn't the question he'd been expecting, but at the same time he should have guessed. Cate picked up the smallest details and never let anything go until she was satisfied. "It's a scuba diving competition. Something like re-enacting war games, but under the water. He won it once and has gone every year since. I think someday he wants to open a dive shop."

"Oh, that's interesting. I'd never expected him to have that kind of passion."

"People run deep." And he certainly had firsthand knowledge of that little gem of wisdom.

Jason turned off I-70 at Silverthorne and pulled into a gas station. "I've gotta make a pit stop. Want some coffee?"

"Yes!"

He laughed at the intensity in that single uttered word. "Still an addict?"

"Still."

"I'll get a couple when I'm in there. Need anything else?"

"Just the coffee."

Jason made his pit stop and bought two coffees. Heading back, he nodded to a couple of teenagers admiring the car, and since Cate was unaware of his approach, gave himself a moment to study the woman inside it.

She still had killer cheekbones.

Richard once said she had a model's face and then had done his best to mold her into his style of eye candy. Her long golden hair had, at Richard's direction, been sheared to a sleek cap. It worked on her, but there wasn't much left to run one's fingers through.

And her usual attire of wools, gabardines, slacks and sweaters, which Jason had named her "Kate Hepburn" wardrobe, as Miss Hepburn was one of Cate's favorite actresses, had fitted his Cate to a T, Richard had replaced with clingy silks, sparkly satins, gowns and dresses.

Richard's choice of couture had certainly showcased her long willowy figure, but then every man could ogle her. Perhaps that was his ex-partner's intent, to show her off as one of his possessions.

Jason shook his head to clear useless memories, none of this was his business any longer. "Here you go." He handed her the double-nested paper cup. "Be careful, it's hot."

He let her take a sip before starting off on the last leg of the trip.

The coffee cup in her hand trembled violently. Snagging it before she spilled any and burned herself, he pulled out the car's hidden cup holder and wedged the cup in.

"I'm doing this all so badly. Ever since Richard's death, I haven't been able to do anything right, and now my baby..." She turned away.

The blame in her voice rubbed him raw. He didn't want to care. He didn't want to worry about her and Haley. He'd wanted a clean break.

Angry at his inner voice, he wrenched the ignition key.

He worked the gears and the car flew down the two-lane road winding through the Blue River Valley. Up and over Rabbit Ears' twisty pass, taking the curves tight and fast, passing and weaving between cars, he made it to the outskirts of Steamboat in record time, grateful there weren't any Colorado Highway Patrol cars lurking about.

"Are we going to the sheriff's department or the house first?" Cate asked, breaking the silence of the past hour.

"House. You okay with that?"

"Exactly what I wanted."

"Keep an eye out for State Highway 20, it'll be a left turn then another left onto... heck, look yourself, it's on the phone." Jason held out the phone for her to see. "You be the navigator."

She took the phone. "Where'd you get this?"

"Anders sent me the map. He doesn't really want us there, but knew he couldn't stop us, so saved us some time."

"Thank you for taking care of Haley and me."

He barely heard her whisper but couldn't miss the spark of heat she ignited when her hand touched his briefly.

"The address shows it's near a Lake Catamount on

Rothsburg Road, in Catamount Estates." Cate looked at him. "Rothsburg? Any connection?"

"I'd guess so. Anders said the Roths' house is yellow with a wrap-around porch."

They passed newly built homes, some sort of club house with a pool and tennis courts, then back to fields and scrub brush.

"That wasn't Catamount Estates. Did we miss it?" Cate squirmed in her seat with anticipation. Knowing Haley wasn't actually there burned another hole in her stomach, but maybe she'd find something that would tell her for sure that Luci had Haley. For despite the assurance she'd proclaimed to Anders and Jason, it was only a gut feeling and she needed proof as much as they did.

"Stop! The phone thingie says we just passed the road." She glanced around, only seeing bales of hay and old equipment.

Jason backed up.

"There." Cate pointed to a sun-whitened sign lying on its side. "Steamboat Springs' only paradise on the lake. Catamount Estates," she read aloud, squinting in the bright sun at the faded sign.

They turned left onto a rutted gravel road and started to climb, passing old power box installations and graded but weed-filled driveways that led to graded but empty lots, indicating a housing development that obviously went bust.

High above the lake on the west-facing slope stood a very dilapidated yellow house. The *only* house in the defunct development.

They rounded the last steep bend. Jason geared down and pressed the accelerator to climb the last rutted stretch, only to see a Routt County Sheriff's SUV pull diagonally across the road, directly in front of the car.

"Damn!" Jason braked hard, skidding on the loose gravel, stopping a few hair-raising inches from the county SUV.

Jason backed the car down the grade a bit and switched off the ignition. "Freakin' idiot."

Cate glanced at him with raised brow. "Ready?"

"Give me a sec, decking him would send me to jail."

The Routt County deputy, whose name tag proclaimed him to be Sgt. Tim Smith, got out and stood at the door of his Ford, arms folded, with a frown running into his wraparound sunglasses.

Jason took a couple of deep breaths and nodded to Cate. They got out of the car and approached the officer.

"You all from Denver?"

Cate bristled but held out her hand. The deputy didn't bother shaking it. "Cate Malloy. Haley is my daughter."

"Jason St. Pierre."

Cate noticed Jason didn't stick out his hand. She nodded up toward the house. "Thank you for checking out the house so quickly. Can we go up?"

"I've been told to take you up, but you can't go inside. Judge hasn't signed the warrant yet."

"But it's been hours."

"Judge is off Mondays. Fishin'. Trying to get him by cell, but we got mountains here that make that difficult."

"Surely you have more than one judge?" Cate asked, not sure if he was pulling her leg or not. And what was causing the hostility radiating off the man?

"One on maternity leave, the other in Hot Springs, 'bout two hours away."

"But—" Cate felt the less than subtle pressure on her back, Jason's warning for her to be cool. "Okay then, Sergeant Smith, lead the way ... please."

The house had great bones, but time and neglect had eaten

away at the wood and stonework. The porch had missing and raised nails; the floor creaked and groaned when they walked around it. The wooden railing was silvered with age, and the stone abutments were dark with tree sap.

Cate was sure she'd be able to spy inside and prove to all that her daughter had indeed been kept captive here. Unfortunately, curtains were drawn over most of the many windows. Still, she peered into each one. In the kitchen, she saw the box of Cheerios and the small TV, still on the Cartoon Network.

"It's killing me that I can't go in there," she said to Jason as she let him have his turn at the window.

"You promised. The warrant will be here soon."

"Not soon enough for me," she said, a tad bit irritated that Jason read her mind so plainly.

At the rear of the house, the porch widened and cantilevered over the ridge. The view to the lake was magnificent and unobstructed. The sun played off the water and Cate swore she saw fish jump, making rings in the crystalline surface.

Multiple glass doors spanned the width of the house, making the most of the view. Cate furtively tried each curtained door to see if any were left unlocked in the Roths hasty departure. But each remained firmly closed.

Sergeant Smith followed them at a few paces distance, as if expecting trouble. Anders had briefed him well, she thought ruefully.

Reaching the final set of glass doors, she found another gap in the curtains. Pressing her body as close as possible to the window, she peered through the gap, seeing paper and crayons on the coffee table, and knew without a doubt Haley had been drawing something.

It tortured her that only a thin pane of glass separated her from being in the same spot her daughter had been only hours before. What had she been drawing? Cate only hoped that when the warrant came and they were able to get a look at the drawing, it would give them another clue.

Fighting the urge to pound on the glass, break it so she could enter, Cate turned away, pausing after she felt a tug and heard fabric rip.

Glancing down at her shorts, Cate realized her pocket had caught on the door.

And as if her wish were being granted, the door was now minutely ajar. This one hadn't been locked!

She bit down her yelp and whirled around to see if Jason or the sergeant had heard her.

Steeling herself to act normal, she moved to the railing to stand by Jason and the deputy, frantically thinking of a way to get rid of them so she could slip in and out of the house in a wink. If she was going to break the law, she wasn't going to take Jason with her.

"It's really gorgeous up here. What happened to the development? This looks like an ideal spot," Jason asked the deputy.

Sergeant Smith jerked his head back toward the house. "Randall Roth, the developer, had a heart attack. He was loaned up to the hilt. The bank took back everything but this house. Mrs. Roth was left with nothing. And Luci, she moved away when she graduated."

The bitterness in Smith's voice was as clear as glass that he'd had tender feelings for Luci Roth. Was there any way Cate could play on that?

The radio on Smith's shoulder crackled to life. "Got any visitors up there yet, Smith?"

"Got the mother and her boyfriend."

Jason and Cate exchanged looks.

"Well, tell her it'll be tomorrow before—" Static broke the radio connection.

"Before what?" Cate asked.

"Dunno." He moved to the edge of the porch. "Jean, come in. Jean, repeat that last part. Jean?"

Sergeant Smith clicked off the radio. "Gotta get the cell. Signal will clear that hill—see the water tank across the lake? Got a cell tower on it."

And he took off.

Cate's eyes grew large; she couldn't help it.

Instinct kicked in and she followed Smith around the porch until she was sure he was headed down to his SUV. Then she ran back to the back of the porch.

"You better follow him, Jason." And pulled open the door wide enough so she could just slip through. Ten seconds, that's all it would take.

"Cate, are you out of your bloody mind?"

"Yes and hush. In fact leave, then you won't be involved."

She zeroed in on her daughter's drawings. There was nothing else of Haley's around, so Cate scooped up the drawings, stuffed them in her shirt and slipped out the door.

Right into the chest of Sergeant Smith.

He yanked her arm behind her, roughly forcing her to her knees.

Jason tried to reach her, but Smith blocked him as he slapped cuffs on Cate. Just as in the movies, the cold steel bit into her wrist.

"Christ, man, have some sympathy. Her daughter has been kidnaped. She just wants her back."

"B&E. You broke the law."

"The door was open," Cate said.

"Can you prove it?"

Cate shook her head at Jason.

"Yes. The door was open." Jason replied.

"Sure. The boyfriend comes to the rescue," Sergeant Smith

sneered. "I'm taking you in. You know the judge isn't here right now, so you'll be spending some time in our quality accommodations. Courtesy of the Routt County Sheriff's Department."

He yanked Cate up by her cuffed hands.

"Careful. You don't have to be rough, she's not a threat."

"Get back or you'll be keeping her company."

"Jason, don't. I need you to keep looking for Haley."

Cate limped to the SUV. Her knees hurt horribly.

Sergeant Smith gave her no assistance into the high vehicle. When Jason moved to help her in, she shook her head.

Falling face first onto the seat, she was forced to twist around and sit up straight. She sent a venomous glare at the sergeant, then stared straight ahead, furious and scared.

How could she continue the search for her daughter from the confines of a jail cell?

4

LAST NIGHT, AFTER SHE'D BEEN FINGERPRINTED, CATE HAD EITHER paced the small holding cell or stared at the ceiling. She hadn't been able to talk to Jason and had imagined every possible worst-case scenario. This morning a female deputy had allowed her to freshen up and then brought her to the judge's chambers.

And now, as the new day dawned bright, she was about to find out just how accurate her imagination was. At least Jason was allowed to be present. She'd never been as grateful for a familiar face as she was at this moment.

She glanced around the small room. It wasn't fancy. The yellowed, pine-paneled walls were dotted with framed diplomas proclaiming Arnold P. Struthers had been awarded this or that degree. Haphazardly placed between the diplomas were autographed photographs of famed skiers from Steamboat. His pine desk was massive but scarred and nicked, as if it had already seen a lifetime with its owner.

Judge Struthers wasn't fancy either. A big bear of a man with a tanned face and brown eyes—deep and unfathomable. His head was crowned by a head of thick black hair. He looked unapproachable.

Cate's heart plummeted to her feet.

"In front of me are two pieces of paper." The judge's voice rumbled out in a rich baritone, perfect for the bench. Not perfect for her.

"One is the charge of Breaking and Entering, with the recommendation of pursuing said charge."

Cate couldn't find the voice to protest, and Jason sat stone still in the only other chair in the office, hands resting on the arms of the old oak chair. A facade, for she felt the tension radiating in waves off his body.

"The other is the search warrant." The judge stared at her, then at Jason and back at her. Surely the judge could hear her frantic heartbeat. Surely she would pass out right at his feet.

Cate forced herself to breathe; going to jail meant she couldn't keep looking for Haley, and when she was found, hold her tight—then keep her tethered to her the rest of her life!

She looked at Jason, knowing he was Haley's only lifeline if she went to jail. "Find her and keep her safe," she begged, then quickly looked back at the judge, and met his eyes squarely and hopefully, bravely.

He nodded and with bold strokes, signed the second paper.

Damn. Just get it over with. By signing the search warrant he was postponing her fate.

"Now it's your turn. Tell me why I shouldn't remand you back to the sheriff's department to be charged with the crime of unlawful entry."

"I thought I was."

"You were detained and fingerprinted, you were not charged."

Light-headed with sudden relief, Cate didn't know whether to cry or laugh: both felt right. At the same time, she knew she was being given the chance to make her case, and sobered, leaning toward the judge in her earnestness to explain.

"I didn't break and enter. It sounds nit-picky and I'm not trying to be. The door *was* open."

"And these?" The judge spread across his desk the drawings Cate took from the Roth house.

"They were proof my daughter had been there. Proof to me that Luci had taken her."

The judge raised his chin and looked straight down his nose at her. Cate's heart stuttered and she felt about two feet tall. He opened his mouth, then closed it and pursed his lips.

Every word she uttered in her defense felt like climbing a mountain slope covered in jagged talus. Each step on the perilous rubble could take her higher or cause an agonizing fall. Nevertheless, she had to present her case.

"I thought I could find something that would tell me where Haley is, was going, something. But the drawings don't make any sense to me. I'm assuming the blue squiggly lines are water since the house overlooks Lake Catamount. But this time there is a man in the picture along with the brunette-haired woman. Haley's telling a story, but I don't understand it." Her voice rose in frustration. She stopped, looked down at her hands gripping the chair arms. Consciously she loosened her grip, closed her eyes for the count of two and then squarely met the judge's piercing gaze once again.

"I'm sorry. I know it's not enough to simply say it. I just want my little girl back, safe with me. Each time we get a clue, it's as if we're one step behind, or Luci is one step ahead."

"There is no proof Luci was there."

Cate bit her lip, arguing wouldn't help her right now.

"You are a talented journalist. You have an instinct that has been proven right more often than wrong."

"You remember my column? It's been years."

"You won the Pulitzer, made Colorado proud."

Nobody had said that to her other than Jason. She studied

the judge while he studied her, as if each was taking measure of the other.

Then the judge looked down and signed the first paper with his bold slash. Cate bit her lip. She was going to jail.

"Bailiff," Judge Struthers boomed.

Jason practically ejected from his seat. Cate put her hand on his arm and pressed down.

A stocky woman of ancient age entered the room.

"Escort Mrs. Malloy and Mr. St. Pierre to the lobby. And release all Mrs. Malloy's personal property back into her possession."

He turned to Cate who sat motionless. "You *are* free to go."

She tried hard to exit in a dignified manner, and almost made it, until she rushed back to the judge and hugged him.

"You might want to stick around Steamboat and see what else the warrant brings to light. Where can we contact you?" Judge Struthers asked.

Jason finally spoke. "Mountain Hearth."

Cate stared at him. Mountain Hearth was a fantasy she'd once confided to him. As a foster child bounced from home to home, she'd dreamed of her own log home with huge stone fireplaces, leather couches, decks all around and a rooftop hot tub to soak in while watching the stars or snowflakes.

Jason met her eyes, an odd defiance glinting in his.

"That's yours?" The judge asked, giving voice to the new tension suddenly enveloping Cate.

Jason nodded with a tight smile.

THE EARLY MORNING SUN HADN'T YET BURNED OFF THE CRISPNESS of the high mountain air. Jason noticed Cate wrap her arms around herself as they walked the short distance from the courthouse to his car. "Cold?"

"That, and nerves."

Jason reached inside the car, grabbed the fleece pullover he'd borrowed this morning from Anna, one of the Mountain Hearth's caretakers, and handed it to Cate. He tried to ignore the catch in his gut as she quickly pulled it on, then hugged it close to her body. Once he would have hugged her tight, warming her with his own heat. Which inevitably led to feeding each other's flames.

She touched his arm. Memories still running hot, he raised his arms to hug her, then realized a nanosecond later what he was doing, and instead scratched his chin.

They were done. Memories had no place in his heart.

"Thanks for thinking about this." Cate nodded down to the pullover. "But then that's what you do, right?"

"What?"

"Think and then act."

He saw her jaw work and knew she was biting the inside of her mouth, a sure sign she was struggling with something.

"*I* didn't think, Jace, I just *did*. That's not me. I could have been sent to jail. I'm not helping her at all."

Stop with the Jace! We're not Cat and Jace anymore. But she was right; her behavior was not Cate-like. She was the consummate observer and researcher, which is why her op-ed pieces were so damn good.

"You did what you did because her disappearance is out of your norm. You're doing what you need to do for Haley."

"Out of my norm? You sound like you've been talking to a psychologist."

"Nope." No shrinks or analysts for him. A glass of wine, or even occasionally a bottle, and a chat with Marta was better medicine. And after the rawness Cate inflicted on him began to heal, there had been many such chats ... and eventually less wine.

"I assumed you'd want to stay in Steamboat until we got the search warrant report?"

He didn't blame her for the double blink, he had abruptly changed the subject, and as astute as Cate was, she knew that discussion was added to the long list of taboo subjects. In fact there really was little for them to talk about.

"You assumed right." Cate slid on her oversized sunglasses, obscuring her eyes, acknowledging closure of that subject.

Jason caught a movement and looked over Cate's shoulder to see Sergeant Smith coming out of the Courthouse, heading their way. "Time to go," he urged, opening the car door for her, almost pushing her in.

"What?" Cate turned around, stiffened, then slid quickly into the seat.

Jason keyed the ignition just as the sergeant stepped in front of the car.

"Judge is a good judge of character. You sure pulled the wool over his eyes." He stared hard at Cate.

"That's insulting, to him," Jason said, wishing at this moment he could gun the car, but the electric car had no "gunning" noise.

Smith had the grace to blush as he met Jason's mocking gaze. "Didn't mean it that way. You know, Luci was really hurt by her daddy's death, blamed it on greedy banks, swore to get back at them, and give her mama back the dignity taken from her. She and I were sweet on each other until ... she changed. Then she had nothing more to do with me, or anyone from here."

"Would you move out of our way?" Jason requested, keeping his voice neutral. No need to incite another arrest.

"In a minute." He turned his attention back to Cate. "Just

thought you should know you're wrong about her. Luci couldn't hurt anything."

Finally, the sergeant stepped aside so they could drive on.

"I thought so. He *is* still sweet on her," Cate said when they were out of earshot.

"Apparently, but I don't think we're wrong. I knew Luci's father got into financial difficulty. She told me up front when she applied to be my assistant, knowing it might be a negative if I found out through the background check. That impressed me. But I didn't probe further, after all it was her father's business, and her check came back clean, as you know from the file.

"And that was my mistake. Obviously her father's bankruptcy was a game changer for her." Jason shook his head, wondering if he was doomed to always misjudge women. So far his track record was zero for two.

"You think Luci took Haley for ransom?"

"Why else?"

THE REMAINDER OF THE DRIVE WAS QUIET.

The powerful car zigzagged up "the mountain," as the locals called the ski area, which in reality comprised several mountains. Up past ski chalets, condos and ski lift houses and further up into the trees. Mountain Hearth soared four stories high, a slim and elegant column, its roof just peeking up past the tree tops for an unobstructed view of the stars.

Six and a half years ago, he'd built Mountain Hearth for Cate, giving life to her dreams.

He'd never set foot in the place until last night.

As Jason pulled into the cobbled circular drive, his caretakers came out to greet them. "Anna, Tom, meet Cate." He turned to Cate. "They look after the place for me."

"Everything you asked for is upstairs. May I park the car for you?"

Jason smiled at the eagerness in Tom's face and flipped him the keys. "Why don't you and Anna take a quick spin while we have some coffee. When you get back, plug it in for me."

The couple grinned, got into the car and headed off.

Jason and Cate were alone, and an awkward silence buzzed between them.

He'd wondered if she was going to give voice to the look she'd flashed at him about the name of the place. He wasn't going to bring it up, and he hoped she'd have the sense not to either.

"How'd you find your caretakers?" Cate asked.

"The Tuckers—Anna and Tom—got married a few months ago and decided to take a year off before heading back to school. They live here in exchange for taking care of everything. They'll ski this winter and apparently wore out their bikes this summer. Then come Spring, they'll go back to England and Oxford, and another couple will come and replace them."

"I wondered about the accent. They seem very nice." Cate nodded toward the open door. "You said something about coffee."

"Coffee *and* chocolate croissants." His reward was a weary smile from Cate.

"Perfect. Missed breakfast at the jail this morning."

Jason held back as Cate wandered through the door into the house of her dreams, chiding himself over suddenly feeling edgy. What the hell did he care whether it lived up to her expectations or not? In fact, she should know just what she was missing.

Despite his rotating caretakers' pleas, saying the house could bring in a couple thousand a night during the height of the ski season, Jason had refused to open it for use. Not even his friends were aware of its existence. In fact, he should have sold it. But he hadn't.

He'd built it as a wedding present for Cate and had planned on honeymooning here. He hadn't planned on her refusing him. *And why should you have?* They'd dreamed and schemed over every part of their life together and were in sync, except for the "having children" part. She wanted to wait, he didn't. Neither of them had been raised in a traditional family, and he desperately wanted to start one.

He shook off the memories; this wasn't the time to relive the past. *No, usually it's the blackest part of the night when you let her haunt you.*

Cate poked around the ground floor, mulling over the house's name. Mountain Hearth was what she'd dubbed her dream house since she was old enough to read through magazines and see that people lived differently than she did— yet here stood a house with her dream name.

But the entry way with its cobbled floor opening up into a large mudroom complete with benches to pull off boots and racks to stow skis wasn't part of her dream.

Despite a silly disappointment that this wasn't "her" Mountain Hearth, the room flooded with filtered sunlight was perfect.

She peeked into a small bathroom and checked inside a couple of the cupboards lining the walls, curious that they were all empty.

Following her nose, the scent of coffee drew her upward, and she climbed the carved wooden spiral staircase. The bannisters were silky smooth, the walls were plastered and painted a warm mocha, working well with the buttery aspen wood and earth-toned cobbles.

The stairs spiraled up and up, opening into the living room with a cathedral ceiling of planked fir. A huge moss-rock fireplace dominated one wall. The opposite wall was made entirely of French doors opening onto the balcony that faced into the forest. Private and magical. Haley would have adored this place, for surely elves and fairies had to be right outside, playing amongst the trees.

She quickly dashed away tears of exhaustion and fear as footsteps signaled Jason was on his way up.

"Coffee's in the kitchen."

Grateful that he ignored her latest bout of waterworks, she followed as he disappeared behind the fireplace into a streamlined ultra-modern galley kitchen.

"Grab the mugs, and I'll take the croissants. I don't trust you with all of them."

Heart heavy, she forced a smile, knowing he was trying to make the moment comfortable for her and himself. They could both play the game of being normal, though he was sure to play it better. He always played all the games better than she did. He used strategy to win. She played by watching and usually losing until she learned. Even now, she mostly lost. Game-playing in life or on a board wasn't her bag.

Closing her eyes briefly, she willed memories away and returned to the game of the moment as she followed Jason back to the living room.

After loading her plate with two sinful croissants, chocolate bits bulging out and smelling like cocoa and butter heaven, Cate chose the leather club chair, toed off her sandals and was about to sit cross-legged until her bruised knees protested. Straightening out her legs, she propped her feet on the corner of the couch Jason wasn't sitting on. Comfortable now, she couldn't decide whether to gulp the coffee first and then eat or just dig in.

The croissant won this battle. Gone in sixty seconds.

Looking at Jason over the rim of her mug, she noticed he hadn't taken much more than a bite from his.

"In case you'd like something more substantial, Anna stocked the kitchen. Eggs, cheese, a couple of steaks and wine. I could make you an omelet if you'd like. Or grill a steak."

Choking on her coffee, Cate waved him away as he came to whack her on the back. "You cook now?"

"Marta taught me."

"You made time for cooking lessons?"

Cate met his intense gaze, refusing to look away.

"It made the nights bearable."

She blinked. He won.

"Speaking of nights, I didn't get much sleep last night in the holding cell. Do you think I have time to take a nap before we hear back about the search warrant results? I want to be brain fresh."

Jason nodded upward. "I think you'd be most comfortable in the suite on the left. If you'd like to shower, I'm sure Anna has all the necessities in there ready to go."

"Is that their suite? I don't want to intrude—"

"My caretakers live in the small cottage we passed on the way up the drive."

Ohhh, he was so good at playing normal, acting as the consummate host at the moment. She grabbed her mug and plate, adding another croissant for good measure, and headed up the stairs, back as ramrod straight as she could make it, the exit effect ruined by her slight limp.

They hadn't fought, not really, but she felt battered. Walking into the suite only added salt to her wounds.

The bed was built from timbers, set high and covered with a thick wool blanket woven with images of deer, raccoon and bear. This was straight out of her dream house.

Jason had remembered.

An adobe beehive fireplace sat empty and cold in the corner, but she could easily imagine it lighted, with flames dancing.

The bathroom was also as she'd once dreamed. Sunken tub big enough for two, though in her youthful dreams, she was the only one covered in bubbles. Rich green granite, mimicking the color of the pine and fir trees outside the window, graced the counters and ledges. The shower was open to the room, glass tiles built into the wall, giving it light from outside.

There was little use in taking a shower if she was only going to put on her old grimy clothes. On impulse, she went back to the bedroom and looked in the drawers of the massive bureau, hoping there would be a T-shirt or something fresh she could borrow. Instead, neatly folded stacks of lacy sexy lingerie with tags still attached, filled the top drawers.

Thoughts of Jason up here with his latest girlfriend painted its uncomfortable image into her brain.

Pulling open the closet she found it mostly empty, with the exception of a few wool sweaters folded on the built-in shelves and a couple of robes hanging in the back. One, a peach silky kimono, the other a black cashmere.

Fierce hot anger wiped any thought of a shower right out of her mind. How dare Jason choose to show her in this fashion that he had other women in his life. She slammed open the door and flew down the spiral steps as fast as she could, bruised knee be damned.

"Couldn't sleep?"

"Nope. Not in a room where you bring your girlfriends. It was cruel to suggest I use that specific room."

"What the hell are you talking about?"

"The bureau filled with lingerie?"

She saw confusion in his gaze, then understanding dawn.

"Yup, that one."

Jason moved like a panther until he stood toe to toe with her. She wanted to back away, but pride and resentment wouldn't let her.

"Did you check the sizes?"

"What? Ewww! Of course not."

"You should have. They are yours. Or I should say I bought them for you. I'd forgotten about them."

"Mine?"

She backed away from him as an awful thought broke through her anger. "When did you build this?"

"A lifetime ago."

He turned and went out to the deck, his stance rigid, dismissing her as surely as if he'd slammed a door shut.

Well screw him—he couldn't just shut her out, not after the bomb he'd dropped.

"Why? Why aren't you pissed at me for being impulsive at the Roth house? Why didn't you just leave instead of sticking around after I was arrested? Why did you build this place? Why?" She yelled at him and didn't care if anyone heard, only knowing that Jason needed to give her answers.

He turned around, brow cocked.

She stood her ground. It was time for this conversation.

"Jace?"

"Cat?"

She winced at the intimate nickname he'd given her. She hadn't heard it in years, and now it was more a slap than a caress.

Jason's smile was grim, but he moved back inside and chose the chair she'd sat in earlier, signaling she take the couch. "Fine, you want me to be pissed? I can be, but don't think you need me to be.

"'One, I think you're going through enough hell with Haley's disappearance. Two, I built Mountain Hearth as a wedding present for you. Three, do you think I'd simply abandon the search for Haley because you decided to act with your heart instead of your head? If so, you don't know me at all. My only goal is to find Haley. Not to taunt you, or hurt you. Fourth and last, we have a past and can't deny it, as much as we might want to."

His words hit her like body blows, and somehow the very last ones, "we have a past," were the worst. She knew it was the simple truth, but it sounded so final, so distant, so finished. *And of course it is. You knew everything was finished the moment you refused his proposal and walked out of the bower of lights and candles he'd created.*

And how could he drop those blows in such an even, conversational tone? *Because it is as he said, it's the past to him. It's easy to lay out the facts when you're no longer emotionally involved.*

Somehow she rose from the couch and made it upstairs to the suite. The huge bed cradled her fall, as the searing pain curled her into a ball.

Sleep wouldn't come. She covered herself with the blanket and still felt chilled.

Richard's death hadn't wounded her as much as Jason's words. She'd killed his love, but not her own.

"Cate?"

She ignored the knock on the door. She hadn't yet figured out how to hide from Jason the painful realization that she still loved him.

"The judge is on the phone."

5

Just as Jason was ready to knock again, Cate swung open the door.

It startled him to see her so wounded, her usually vibrant green eyes dull and flat. Her skin wan under her tan and her shoulders slumped. He'd been honest when she demanded answers, but he didn't think he'd been brutal.

Not brutal, maybe a bit heartless, even cold.

Ignoring the truth of his inner voice, Jason put the phone on speaker.

"She's here."

"Just so you both know, the sheriff gave me permission to report what was found at the Roth house." Judge Struthers's deep voice boomed over the phone's tiny speaker.

"We appreciate it," Jason said.

"What did they find?" Cate asked simultaneously.

A deep, brief chuckle rang through the speaker. "The house was pretty empty. Clothing, food, and only two of the bedrooms had furniture. As I said, the rest of the house was mostly empty and appeared to have been that way for some time. They found several clothing tags for shorts, T-shirts and nightwear in the

trash for a child's size six, along with a large shipping box from
the Cherry Creek Neiman Marcus, sent more than a week ago
and addressed to Luci at your Morrison address, St. Pierre."

The judge paused.

"While I'm not a cop, this feels premeditated to me. The
sheriff here is in touch with Chief Anders."

"Who's going to follow up on the Neiman Marcus angle?"
Jason asked.

"Anders. The only car in the garage was Mrs. Roth's, with a
dead battery. So they left using someone else's. We're guessing
Luci's, and as you know, there's already an ABP out on it."

"So you believe me about Luci?" Cate asked.

"Your instincts are playing out as evidence points in her
direction. The question remains, why?"

"Yeah, and I can't imagine the answer," Cate said.

"I truly hope you find your daughter soon, Mrs. Malloy."
And then they heard the click of disconnect.

Jason switched off the speaker on his phone.

"I guess we wait again until Luci's Jeep is found," Cate said,
frustration lacing each word.

"I don't think we can do more until we know her next move."

"I think—"

"Do you think—"

Despite himself, he smiled as again they spoke
simultaneously. Cate didn't smile. Yet he knew she remembered
it was a common occurrence; the memory played in her eyes.

"You first," he offered.

"I think we should head back to Morrison. I'm sure Luci isn't
sticking around here. I can pick up my car at your place—well,
after I get it jumped or a new battery, and then wait for news at
my apartment. Anders has my phone number."

That wasn't what he expected her to say, though he should
have. Wanting to hunker down, think on the problem, use the

solitude to regroup. Her rash behavior was an anomaly. *But then, so was having your daughter kidnapped.*

"Running away isn't going to work, Cate."

Her back straightened and the wounded look fled her eyes, replaced by the spark of anger, and oddly, a flicker of unease.

"Running away? From finding my daughter?"

"No, from me."

Cate stared at him, dumbfounded. *How could he know, when she herself just realized she was still in love with him?* She wanted to duck back into the bedroom and hide, embarrassed that he had so obviously moved on after their break up and she hadn't.

"We're together in this until Haley is back with you. I know you need clothes," he said. "We can stop by the apartment and get them, but you're not staying anywhere alone. I have plenty of room at my place—you can be as alone as you need to be. It could take awhile to track down the Jeep."

Thank goodness, he doesn't know. Relief barely registered as Cate felt her world tilt again. "Oh my God! I didn't call my new job. I'm a no-show."

"I'll call them and explain."

"No, you won't."

Limping down the spiral stairs as fast as she could to the living room, she found her purse and her journal. Dialing the Post's office, she headed out to the deck to make the call. If she was going to be fired, she didn't want Jason to see her failure.

Walking back into the living room after the brief call, she noticed the questioning concern on Jason's face. It irritated her. She just wanted to be alone with her misery, not have to explain what was happening.

"Cate?"

"They gave me until the end of the week. They were sympathetic, 'but they need to move on finding someone else to write the *About Town* column if I can't commit,'" she quoted. "Commit? I can't commit to anything until I have Haley back."

"Wait a sec. You're going to write the *About Town* column for the Post? You'd rather pull out your eyeballs than write that stuff."

"Beggars can't be choosers."

"Come again?"

"Nothing. Is the car charged? Can we leave?"

She saw him retreat into his polite social demeanor once more, which was just bloody fine. It would make the trip back easier.

"Of course. Let me call Tom and have him bring up the car."

No, the trip back would be horrible. "Jason? I'm sorry."

He turned and gave her a cool look. "No problem, let's get going."

Right, no problem. They were back to being polite strangers. Maybe it was best after all.

"I had to take that job. It was the only one that wanted me."

Jason stopped mid-step down the staircase. "Cate, you're a Pulitzer Prize-winning journalist. In fact—"

"Except now I'm a mother first, and all choices are based on that. Plus, I haven't written or been in print for six years."

That gut-slammed him. Hadn't that been what he'd asked of her, and she fled?

He finished the step down and took another one. Damn her, damn her to hell.

He kept moving down, fighting the urge to run, to take out his anger on the road, legs pumping and heart pounding.

"I had to take the job."

He barely heard her and used that as an excuse to ignore her.

"I'm broke," she yelled, as if making sure he heard this one. "Surely you knew that."

"Richard was making some odd investments when we dissolved the firm, but he wasn't broke. Did you shop him into poverty?" He winced as the shouted words left his mouth, but he couldn't take them back now.

"You read the tabloids now? And believe them?"

"I know what I saw. Designer gowns, brilliant jewels and that damned arsenal of cars you owned."

"All for show. I was arm candy, the mother of his beautiful daughter. Highgate and the car collection were trappings, like gilt painted on. I sold everything to pay his debts."

He certainly hadn't been expecting that to come out of her mouth.

Pivoting, he climbed up the stairs to face her. He needed to see her eyes. Cate couldn't lie without a telltale twitch in her right eye. "Debts? And the Malloys didn't offer to help?"

"They blamed me, much as you just did."

No twitch.

"I noticed you kept the Subaru and are renting an apartment, not buying a smaller place."

"All I could afford. I'm not using Haley's trust, and anyway I'd have to petition the trustees, and that I'm never doing. I have three thousand left. The first and last month's rent took a chunk, so you see, I had to take that job."

She swept past him on the stairs, relieved at least that part of the story was out in the open. Not the whole story, but enough to make Jason realize she had little to fall back on. Hell, nothing to fall back on. And while she'd been poor before, she'd been single. Now everything was different.

Not true, now everything was simply dark again.

The job had been a tiny sliver of light, allowing her and Haley to start anew. A job that would allow her to get some writing creds back and reestablish herself as a good writer. They wouldn't have been in the small apartment forever.

Now, her entire world was focused on simply getting Haley back. Then they'd take the next step together.

Cate stopped and looked up the stairs, surprised Jason hadn't followed her to continue the argument. He changed before her eyes. The anger, the rigid stance fled, an uncharacteristic uncertainty taking its place.

"I've never lied to you, Jason." She knew he'd been looking for her twitch, and she also knew he hadn't found it. It was the truth. Nobody knew Richard had debts that amounted to the bills of a small city. *Nobody but the Malloys, and now Jason.*

Cate hadn't been aware of any of it until after his death when the lenders and shops started contacting her and she'd realized the checkbook was nearly empty.

She hadn't wanted the gowns, the jewels or the house. To be comfortable, yes. To be able to give Haley adventures and the special treats Cate never had. But to be overtly ostentatious, no.

Richard believed with all his heart that the trappings of wealth showed the world he wasn't only the prodigal son to the Malloy heritage, that he could do it one better himself.

Perhaps she should have paid more attention to their finances. *But why? Jason had done amazingly well—why shouldn't Richard have done as well?*

Cate shook her head to rid herself of such useless thoughts. The only "why" that mattered now was why Haley had been kidnapped by Luci Roth. Who apparently wanted ransom from a broke woman. Or from Haley's trust.

"So, now that you know that sordid little detail, if you'd drop me off at the apartment, I'll wait there to hear from Anders."

"Nothing's changed, Cate. I'm in this until Haley is back with you. And as much as I'd rather be at my house than sleep on the couch at your apartment, I'll do that if you insist on staying there."

A dark chuckle escaped before she could shut it down.

His raised brow demanded she explain. "I was imaging you hanging over each arm on the love seat, as it's the only couch that would fit in the place."

It would be easier to avoid him, to hide her feelings for him at his house than at her one-bedroom place.

"Okay, your house wins."

6

———

CATE'S NEW NEIGHBORHOOD WAS TYPICAL MIDDLE AMERICAN AND comforting. Kids playing outside on this August afternoon filled the air with laughter, and elderly couples sitting on their porches nodded hello as he drove slowly past.

It wasn't a neighborhood of high-profile parties or police reports. She'd chosen well for Haley.

The apartment building itself was better than Jason envisioned after seeing the old worn key she'd handed the movers. It was small and, by its simple block architecture, built in the 40s, but it was neat and smelled of the soft summer Colorado breeze and fresh cut grass.

The movers had wrangled in Haley's armoire, but left it in the middle of the small living room, making it nearly impossible to get to the bedroom. So he waited by the front door as Cate grabbed what she needed.

An elderly woman climbed the stairs spryly and gave him a bright smile. "Is Mrs. Malloy inside? I'm Barbara, her landlady. I have her spare key the movers gave me."

Jason grasped the wrinkled hand she held out. "She's inside."

"Barbara, is something wrong?" Cate asked, stepping out of the apartment, a small suitcase in hand. She firmly closed the door behind her.

"No, no. Just checking to see how you're doing and if you needed a hand keeping little Haley busy while you settled in. Is she at daycare already?"

Jason followed Barbara's questioning glance to the closed apartment door and back to Cate.

Silence lengthened for such a simple question.

"I don't know where she is."

Those agonizing words, torn from Cate's throat, renewed Jason's vow to do whatever was necessary to find Haley and make Luci pay.

"Haley was apparently taken, kidnapped, just before Cate was ready to leave," Jason explained, knowing Cate couldn't get out another word.

"Oh, dear Lord." Barbara covered Cate's hand with her own. "What can I do to help?"

"You haven't seen anything unusual, have you?" Jason asked.

"Thought nothing of it until now, but yes, there was a man coming around with a camera, and one of those video cameras as well, taking all sorts of pictures. I asked him what he was doing, and he said he worked for some realty company interested in buying the place. I told him it wasn't for sale.

"He kept asking questions about kids in the apartment, and except for Haley, I have none, but didn't tell *him* that. He mentioned something about the neighborhood living on the fringe of gang territory and I told him we had a good Neighborhood Watch, and it was past time he left."

"Do you often have Realtors coming around?"

"Nope, that's why his visit hovered in my mind. I have his card, was going to throw it away, but something kept me from doing that. I'll run and fetch it."

Jason took the small suitcase from Cate and guided her down the stairs. If revealing the news about Haley to an outsider was as difficult for Cate to hear as it was for him to tell, he knew her wounds were freshly opened.

Barbara returned with the card. "Kaplan Real Estate, specializing in commercial properties. I just looked 'em up—nothing listed in the phone book." She handed the card to Jason.

"What did this guy look like?"

"Six feet plus, blond hair, receding hairline, my guess for age would be around forty."

Cate clutched his arm. "That sounds like Mark. Jace, do you think he tipped off Luci and that's why she left Steamboat in such a hurry?"

Fury flared deep inside Jason. Was it possible that two of his trusted *and* vetted employees could be involved in such an appalling crime? "Do you mind giving the sheriff in Morrison a description of the man?" he asked Barbara.

She pulled out another card. "Here's my phone number, have 'em call me." Barbara turned to Cate. "And please, let me know when you find Haley. We're all looking forward to having her here, liven it up a bit, you know. In fact we thought we might be her daycare, full time until school starts, and then watch her after kindergarten until you get home. Remember old man Wilson? That was his idea. I think he might even miss her more than me."

"I'm sure we'd both love that." Cate hesitated a moment, then hugged the older woman.

Jason knew, though she wouldn't admit it, that Barbara could fast become the mother figure Cate had never been privileged to have.

His phone buzzed. He glanced at the number and took the call. "Anders," he said by way of greeting, looking at Cate as he said it. The hope flaring in her eyes was almost too much to see. "Hold on, I'm going to put you on speaker."

Barbara moved a few steps away, obviously intent on giving them privacy, until Cate caught her arm. "Thank you for making Haley and me feel so welcome."

"You let me know as soon as you can." Barbara patted her arm and moved back inside her cottage, situated at the front of the small apartment building.

Anders's voice boomed over the phone's speaker. "Found Luci's Jeep at Rocky Mountain Airport. The foursome—"

"Four?" Jason nodded to Cate. "Cate nailed it. Mark's gotta be the one that tipped off Luci. Call Barbara at 303-555-1212—she's the manager at Cate's new apartment—and listen to her description of a man who was nosing around, asking odd questions and using an alias. The description fits Mark."

"No need. It was Mark Adams, he's on the passenger list," Anders said. "The pieces are beginning to gel. Luci had booked commercial for Sunday, but once the Amber Alert came out, she apparently cancelled the flight and booked a charter for this morning to Hawai'i. Honolulu to be exact."

"Honolulu?" Cate repeated. "That I never expected. Do you think there's any reason to think Helene and Harve are involved?"

"They don't strike me as people who'd want to go to jail by helping a kidnapper," Jason said.

"Yeah, but Richard was their only son. On the other hand, nothing is stopping them from coming to Colorado to see Haley any time they wanted," Cate said. "So we're back to why would Luci do this? Unless she wanted ransom from Haley's trust."

"We're thinking along the same lines," Anders said. "My first thought was a ransom pickup from the Malloys, then flee. I bluntly asked your father-in-law if he'd been contacted for a private ransom demand, and he told me specifically that Luci hasn't been in touch with them since this started. I think other than what we've told them, they know little, and they appear to be very concerned for Haley's welfare.

"We did find that Luci paid for the charter, put it on her credit card, and that she also paid for the Neiman Marcus clothes. You *do* pay well, St. Pierre."

"She'll have a hard time spending anything in prison, unless it's for lawyers."

"Well, I gotta tell you, the deeper we dig, the less we know, but here's what we have set up on the Honolulu end, and believe me, the timing was close. We got the charter company to contact the pilots and let them know what was going on, and he's slowing down the jet. It'll land in about ten minutes. I've already alerted Honolulu PD that Haley's an Amber Alert. The pilots won't be surprised when the police meet the plane. Cate, I think you'll agree there is no reason for Haley to go to Social Services if she has family to be with instead, so I've arranged for the Malloys to pick up Haley. Luci, her mother and Mark will be taken into custody. I'll let you know as soon as I know anything more concrete." He clicked off.

Cate looked at Jason. "I've got to call Helene and Harve, and have them bring Haley back immediately."

"Hold on a sec. How many days of clothing did you pack?"

"A couple, why?"

"Luci isn't the only one who can charter a jet. Let's go get Haley."

He wasn't ready when Cate launched herself at him and nearly knocked him over.

THE PREMIERJET PASSENGER LOUNGE AT CENTENNIAL AIRPORT fitted the elite customers they catered to. Soft gray wool carpet, maroon leather club chairs, and glass desks with Wi-Fi. A massage and shower room. Even a sleep room.

Floor-to-ceiling windows showcased the sun's long descent into evening behind the rugged mountains to the west.

Cate stood against one of the windows and tried to let relief soothe away the fear of the last few days. Shortly she would be reunited with Haley. Luci's charter pilot knew what was going on, as did the HPD. There was no way she could slip away from them this time.

Calling her in-laws several times over the past hour was proving to be an exercise in futility as the phone simply rang and rang, didn't go to voicemail, wasn't forwarded, just rang.

She took comfort in Jason's theory that Helene and Harve were lying low to avoid the media. If word got out that the Malloys' grandchild was a kidnap victim, it could become a media circus, worse than Richard's funeral.

The crew Jason requested hadn't arrived yet, and Jason had his phone glued to his ear, conferring with Marta over a couple of important deals he wanted her to monitor until they returned.

It felt odd, to be close to putting an end to at least this part of the nightmare, yet just waiting, not doing anything. And there would be more waiting, almost seven hours on the jet. While she was pleased that kidnapping charges would be brought against Luci and most likely Mark, she was worried about what a trial would do to Haley. Did children have to be witnesses on the stand? And how did Mrs. Roth fit into this?

So, while the nightmare would continue for her, at least until Luci and Mark were behind bars, she'd have Haley and would do her best to make sure her daughter didn't suffer through the messy cleanup of this ordeal.

Jason, phone in hand, came over. "Just got a text from

Anders, Haley is with her grandparents, the gang of three was taken by HPD."

He looked up from the tiny screen and she saw just a sheen of tears in his whiskey brown eyes. "The worst is over, Cate, and you'll have Haley in your arms before midnight."

Not caring whether it was appropriate or not, Cate held on to Jason and let her tears fall silently. She had no idea how long they stood. It could have been seconds or minutes. Finally she pulled away as a PremierJet's attendant approached them.

"The crew you requested have arrived. About forty-five minutes and you're on your way. We just put out the dinner buffet if either of you is hungry."

Arm in arm, they wandered over to the cold buffet. Cate nibbled on orange slices and avocado-stuffed wontons, Jason absently grabbed at one thing or another and ate it while back on the phone with Marta.

But more than food, Cate craved a warm shower. She needed to get the feel of jail off, and she'd been wearing the same clothes for the past two days. She wanted to be clean, and now that Haley was safe, a shower to remove all physical traces of her side of the ordeal felt imperative.

She touched Jason, pointed at her watch and the shower room.

He nodded and winked as his lips slowly curved upward into his crooked smile.

Her heart stuttered. Cate did her best to ignore it by reminding herself it was simply Jason's smile—it was always crooked and sexy. *But he doesn't wink at everyone and his smile doesn't reach his eyes with everyone.*

Arguing with herself didn't help her rapid heartbeat, and she fled to the sanctuary of the shower room.

The limestone-tiled shower had a myriad of soaps and

razors, shampoos and shave cream to choose from. The towels, folded in a warming cabinet, were only a reach away.

Cate turned the water on hot and hard, relishing the pounding spray. For the first time in years as she soaped her body, she wondered just how different she'd look to Jason from the Cate of old. She'd had a child, her hips felt wider, her breasts heavier.

As she used a razor on her legs, she was pleased they were still lean and strong, more than capable of wrapping around him and drawing him in deeply.

Alarmed at the sensual and completely inappropriate direction of her thoughts, she closed her eyes and let the water sluice down her, trying to rinse off the aching need Jason awakened deep inside her.

THE JET WAS SLEEK AND COMFORTABLE. FRANK, THEIR SILVER-haired pilot, introduced himself, then finished his preflight with Dani, a younger, female co-pilot.

She turned in her cockpit seat to face them. "It's a little more than a seven-hour flight tonight. Dinner and drinks are in the galley. You know the drill, Mr. St. Pierre. The tower just cleared us, so if you'll quickly stow the bag and fasten your belts, we'll go," Dani instructed.

Jason smiled his thanks.

"Already? I thought we'd have a bit more time before takeoff."

"Cate, it'll be fine. Frank flew for the Air Force, then commercial, and Dani flew in Iraq. You can't get much better than these two. Father and daughter. I try to always get them for my crew."

She glanced at the cockpit, impressed. Still she was grateful when he quickly pulled her seatbelt snug and locked the leather captain's chair so it wouldn't swivel or rock.

The jet revved and vibrated, its engines held back until the last moment, then it sped down the tarmac, lifting smoothly into the twilight, and banked to the West.

Jason was right, it was okay, but flying, especially the take-off, was on her least enjoyable things-to-do list. She wished she'd grabbed Hippity out of her bag so she could white-knuckle the stuffed bunny. Her daughter would be laughing at her. Haley loved to fly, go anywhere, as long as her mommy or daddy were with her.

"I just don't get it."

"What don't you get?" Jason asked.

"Haley loved to go places, but only if Richard or I were with her."

"She came over to my house often the past six months."

"That's different, your house was like our house. She knew everyone there. She felt safe and happy there." Cate knew her words were true. "But she wouldn't just leave and go somewhere unknown with Luci."

"She trusted Luci."

"We all did—how stupid is that?"

"It's easy to be fooled."

Cate ignored the comment, knowing it was layered with subtext.

"You can unfasten your belts, now," Dani called from the flight deck.

Jason unbuckled, then unbuckled her and moved to a cabinet in the middle of the seating area. He opened the lid and dropped down the front to reveal a fully stocked bar. "Want a cocktail or wine?"

"You choose."

"Mai Tais in honor of the destination."

She wandered over to the small bar and watched as he poured mixer and rum into a glass pitcher, then added precut pineapple spears and ice to each of their glasses, filling them to the brim with the drink.

She took one and was about to sip when Jason lightly clinked his glass to hers.

"To Haley. Aloha."

"I thought aloha meant hello."

"And goodbye, I love you, I like you, and a few other meanings."

"Very handy word." *I love you.* She could say aloha and mean it. When Jason used aloha, it would be one of the other meanings.

While she chewed on the rum-soaked pineapple spear, Jason opened a package of macadamia nuts and poured them in another glass. She took a handful and headed back to her chair. Changing her mind, she made a small detour to the luggage bin and retrieved Hippity from her bag.

"There are a few movies aboard and the latest magazines. I need to make another call."

"I don't need to be entertained. Do your thing."

And before she could reach her seat, Jason was beside her, cupping her cheek in his palm. "I was trying to distract you. I'm going to call a guy I know in Honolulu, Gus Tanaka. He's the best PI on the island."

"Why a private investigator?"

"Why did Luci take Haley?"

Cate felt the alcohol chew on her already knotted up stomach. "That's the million-dollar question, and I have no clue, unless it was the ransom angle."

"Exactly. I want a clue, and Gus is the guy to find them. Do you want to listen?"

Jason saw her nod and pressed the speaker. He dialed and

waited through several rings until a voice said, "Gus Tanaka Investigations."

"Gus, answering your own calls these days?"

"It's late, and only people like you have this number. It's good to hear your voice. What's up, bro."

"En route to HNL, got a case for you. Got time?"

"For you, always."

Jason gave him the facts, and sat back to listen to what the best PI in the country had to offer.

"I'll get surveillance on the Malloys right away. Hold a minute."

Soft Hawaiian background music played as Jason watched Cate worry the ring on her right finger.

"Bro, I've got two men on the house until you get here," Gus said, back on the line. "I remember Richard Malloy's funeral. It was a zoo, huge media event. Even helicopters. You didn't come."

"I wasn't invited. When you fall out with a Malloy, it's forever."

"Good to remember. Richard had a wife. I'm assuming she's with you?"

"Yeah, she's listening."

"I can tell it's on speaker," Gus said with a touch of amusement in his voice. "Mrs. Malloy—"

"Cate, please."

"Cate, we'll do our best to find out why Ms. Roth and company decided it was a good idea to kidnap your daughter and bring her here. I'm not sure Chief Anders has it right about the ransom. Time to start digging deeper. Jason, I'll meet your plane—you still flying PremierJet?"

"Yes."

"Then I'll find you. Aloha, bro." Gus clicked off.

Jason glanced again at Cate. She continued to worry the ring. "Pretty ring."

"Haley picked it out when she and Richard were shopping at Cherry Creek a few years back." She held up her hand, showing him the garnet and diamond ring shaped like a flower with green tsavorite garnet leaves. "I don't know if you knew this ... I'm not sure how much you and Richard talked, after ... anyway, Richard adored Haley, and she adored her daddy. They would play and make up stories, and he'd always check with her before he ever bought me a present. They were shopping for my birthday, and Haley told him this was the one, because it 'looked like Mommy.' It's the only thing he gave me I kept. Haley likes me to wear it. She misses her daddy so much."

"And you?" He watched intently as she took a sip of her drink, looked at Hippity, everywhere around the cabin, except at him.

"I don't think this is the best time to start this conversation, Jace," she said softly.

He hated the jealousy that suddenly twisted his gut. He hated that Richard had a single redeeming quality. Hated that he had created a family, something Jason had always coveted. Hated that Cate gave *his* dream to Richard. And it galled him that she had no idea how her words wounded him.

Now he was stuck 15,000 feet in the air, in an aluminum tube with nowhere to run from her words. She was right, this wasn't the time. There wasn't a time. Period.

He watched as she cuddled Hippity, rocking back and forth in the chair.

"We've got a bit of turbulence coming up. You might want to stow the drinks, Mr. St. Pierre, and dinner will have to wait," Dani reported over the intercom.

Cate blanched and fumbled with the seatbelt, dropping the stuffed bunny.

Jason buckled her in, looked at the half-finished drinks, bolted hers, then stowed the glass. Glancing at her white-knuckling the arms of the chair, he grabbed a blanket and a mini dop-kit from the overhead compartment above the bar.

He handed her a blanket and the kit. "This'll help. Eye mask and headphones. Beethoven is on channel six."

He knew he sounded harsh and abrupt and tried to soften his tone, making amends by picking up the bunny and handing it to her.

"Thanks, Jace. Good pilots or not, I hate this."

The jet lurched, not enough to bother him, but Cate hastily put on the blackout mask and headphones. She tucked the blanket around her and Hippity. "Channel six?"

"Yup."

Then he watched her until her fingers relaxed on the arm rests and her breathing steadied. He downed his drink, put the glass away and rued that he couldn't fix another.

As infuriated as he was, he was a fool to think memories of Cate would dull with time or separation. A fool to think that when she moved from Highgate, out of sight would also mean out of mind.

For the past three days, from the moment she'd slid into his car, everything she said or did brought forth another time when their lives were intertwined.

Where would they end up after they returned to the mainland with Haley? They'd now gone beyond merely being civil to each other because of business needs of the past six years. The desire they'd felt from the day they'd met still simmered. *And that's all it is, old man, hot desire, a need to possess her body once again. Nothing more than that. So stop analyzing it to mean anything other than lust.*

He answered his own question.

There was nothing to rekindle. No future life together. So he'd best remember that. He'd help them both, and then he'd move on with his life. Try to balance work with life.

He had even started a foundation, following in his own way the likes of Bill Gates, Warren Buffet and Bono. He wasn't famous, though he was fairly well known, and while he didn't have billions to pour into it, he had millions. And who was he going to leave it to?

Glancing over at Cate, her fingers totally lax, her chin resting on her chest, she finally was getting the sleep she so needed.

He turned down the cabin lights and worked his phone. Checking on the competition, looking at spreadsheets and evaluating potential businesses to buy into or buy wholly, he buried himself in work. It was the only way at the moment to get the woman an arms-length away, out of his mind.

7

WITH THE LAST OF DAYLIGHT GONE, THE JET LANDED SMOOTHLY AT Honolulu International Airport and taxied to the inter-island terminal adjacent to the main terminal. Cate glanced out the jet's window, recalling the only other time she'd been to Hawai'i was for Richard's funeral, and then she'd only stayed on the island for less than forty-eight hours before she and Haley were back in the air, bound for home and their new life. Neither that visit nor this was turning out to be the traditional fun-in-the-sun vacation people dreamed of when traveling to the islands."

"Don't forget to set your watches back four hours. It's 10:12 Hawai'i time," Dani called from the cockpit.

Jason pointed out his window toward the two nondescript cars topped with light bars waiting by the terminal, their blue LEDs flashing. "I'm guessing those are Honolulu PD detectives. And can you see the skinny guy leaning against the Mustang convertible? That would be Gus."

Cate shook her head in disbelief. "Quite a welcoming party. The last and only time I was here, a white hearse met the plane. Now it's police and a PI." She glanced at Jason, took in his somber brown eyes, and realized just how ungrateful she sounded. "I'm sorry, I don't mean to whine, it's just this whole thing had been so confusing, so bizarre."

"No need to apologize. Someday I hope you'll come back and be met with nothing more than an orchid lei."

A smile curved her lips even as her brows lifted in skepticism.

The jet rolled to a stop, the ground crew placed chocks under the tires, and once set, Dani opened the door. The blast of humid air mixed with jet fumes and fragrant blossoms was a curious, yet totally believable mix—modern Hawai'i

Dani pushed the button to lower the stairs as the trio of men approached the plane.

Jason grabbed her bag from stowage, and Cate clutched Hippity tighter. Very soon, her daughter would again hold her precious bunny.

Cate and Jason shared a smile over the incongruous appearance of the men. Gus, a short Asian decked out in trim khakis and a muted Hawaiian shirt was flanked by the two detectives, massive and tall, looking like NFL linebackers in suits.

Cate saw Gus look up. Apparently he noticed Jason's and her smiles. "Meet Detectives Kevin Watanabe and Ken Watanabe. My cousins."

Cate couldn't believe Jason actually snorted.

"Cousins?"

"Yeah, bro, on my wife's side. Thought we could use them if we needed a bit of official backup."

The twin detectives had yet to say a word, standing still as statues, hands clasped in front of them, legs slightly apart. They looked more like protection services than cops, but then, Cate realized, that's exactly what their job was for the moment, and she was glad they were on her side.

Cate made quick work of the steps, shifted Hippity to her left arm and extended her hand. "Thank you both. I hope we won't need you, but I'm glad you're here. You too, Gus. Jason says you're a genius."

Kevin and Ken coughed loudly, and Gus just shook his head. "'*ohana*," he said in a resigned tone.

"'ohana?"

"Family," Kevin explained and smiled widely. "Mostly it's good."

Gus cuffed him on the arm, and Cate liked them all immediately.

"Maybe not so much genius, for the moment. Even with these two on the inside," Gus pointed to his cousins, "there is nothing on Luci Roth. Nothing. The three were taken into custody but apparently not booked, at least for the moment. And the chief isn't talking, nor are the patrol men who had them."

"What? She kidnapped my daughter."

"We'll find out, one way or the other. Let's go get Haley. It's not too late, and my guys report the Malloys' lights are still on."

"Here's how we'll work this," Ken said. "You two go in first, followed closely by Gus, while we flank you from a distance. Just be a presence. I want you to get your daughter, say thank you and leave. Forget any bags, any toys. The less said the better. Sound okay?"

"Why so rushed?" Jason asked.

"I don't like being kept in the dark about anything, so until I know what the Luci angle is, and why it's so hush-hush, let's just be Teflon—slide in, get Haley and slide out," Gus said, all smiles gone.

Cate nodded, a sick lump blocking any words. This sounded more difficult than simply opening her arms and having Haley run to her. But Gus was right, there were unknowns.

"Then let's roll."

The detectives led the way out of the airport, followed by Gus's Mustang, top still down. The fresh air felt good. Jason wanted her to sit up front, but she wanted the backseat. Excitement and dread coursed through her, both leaving her slightly sick to her stomach. Haley was only minutes away.

They moved fast on Hı, the HPD lights working their magic even at this late hour. Finally they turned off the highway down Hunakai Street toward the ocean.

"You've been to Malloys' house before," Gus asked loudly over the wind of the convertible.

"No—" Cate started, only to be interrupted by Jason.

"Yeah, a few times when I was here for meetings. They'd have a dinner here or at their club."

"I didn't know you knew them that well," Cate said, a bit stunned by this news.

"I don't know them well, but Richard was my partner, so it was purely a social thing when I was here."

"Haley drew blue wavy lines—is the house on the beach?" Cate asked.

"Yeah, they got beach access," Gus chuckled. "This area is called Diamond Head, and it's a big bucks area, probably the richest, and your family's one of the top dogs."

"Not my family," Cate said sharply. She wasn't a Malloy, never had been, but Haley was half Malloy and half Hemstead.

However, in Cate's heart of hearts, she didn't want her daughter to become any more Malloy. "But if the house is on the beach and Haley drew two tall brunette-haired people, she must have known she was coming to Hawai'i ."

"More questions, no answers yet," Gus said.

But Cate heard the uncertainty in his voice, even over the wind.

There was little activity so late as they turned onto Kahala

Avenue. The detectives pulled their cars to the edge of the road. Gus pulled across the driveway.

"We've got it now, clear to leave." Gus spoke into the mic/earphone piece he wore.

Two men in the car opposite the driveway gave Gus the "hang loose" sign and drove off, gunning their car.

"Boys," he sighed and laughed. "They see a blonde *haole* and have to show off. Are you ready?"

Of course she was. Haley was only feet away!

The iron gate decorated with huge verdigris metal-work banana leaves was open, surprising if they were trying to exclude media. But then Luci wasn't charged, so there wasn't a record for a reporter to check on.

Strategic lighting illuminated the garden, and the soft glow of lanterns outlined the brick-laid driveway that curved toward the front door of the estate. The grass was manicured, and the birds-of-paradise flowering high on their stalks seemed to turn and watch as she, Jason and Gus approached the house.

Suddenly, the front door burst open and Haley raced down the steps and flew along the driveway. "Mommy, Mommy! You came. I knew you would."

Cate raced to meet her daughter, knelt on the sharp bricks and hugged Haley hard against her, inhaling the scent of her little girl in pj's, smelling sweetly of a bath and powder.

She nuzzled her nose into the softness of her daughter's neck, not completely believing she was finally holding her baby. "Who cut your hair, little one?"

"Grandmother. She said it was messy."

"We'll let those bangs grow back out, okay?"

"Okay, Mommy. I missed you so much. I love you."

"And I always love you back more."

Jason picked up Hippity, dropped when Cate raced to her daughter. Dusting off the bunny, he waited next to Gus, not wanting to intrude on the reunion, disgusted with himself for feeling left out. Yet he ached at the sight of the two blonde heads together, touching forehead to forehead, and the sound of giggles as they chattered.

Finally Cate turned her head and met his gaze. Her green eyes glimmered with tears, yet shone with happiness. She held out a hand to him, signaling him closer, sucking the breath right out of him. Images of them as a family spun their way into his heart.

He knelt to be on Haley's level. "I think Hippity has missed you," he said as he handed the little girl her bunny.

She squealed and hugged the bunny tightly.

His heart melted again at the shy smile Haley flashed him. "Did you come with my mommy?"

"I did. Are you ready to come home?"

"With Mommy and you?"

"Yup." He met Cate's gaze over Haley's head and saw something flicker in her eyes before she looked down. Maybe it was Haley's "with Mommy and you" that made him consider for a second that Cate harbored the same insane thoughts of them as a family.

He ruthlessly cut those images out of his mind. They could never be a family. Cate had made sure of that.

"Can we go now? Grandmother has too many rules, and my room is yellow. I like pink. And I've been to the doctor and I don't like bangs," Haley said, her tone earnest in the way only a child can sound.

"No, Haley, you may not." Helene Malloy commanded.

Jason stared at the immaculate couple standing in their front door. The Malloys commanded attention if not respect with their regal air and perfectly attired presence.

"Haley, come here, now."

"But Mommy is here. Luci promised we'd be together after she came."

"No whining. Luci misspoke. And please give that dirty bunny back to your mother."

Cate slowly stood. "You will not speak to my daughter that way." She picked up Haley and pivoted. "Jace, we've got to leave," she said in a low, panicked undertone.

Jason saw the confusion and fear in her eyes. "Gus?"

Gus nodded. "Now," he said softly into his microphone.

Everything happened at once. Gus stepped in front of Haley and Cate. Jason stood with him. Kevin and Ken moved in behind Cate and Haley.

"Go quickly," Gus commanded, handing Jason the keys to his Mustang.

Jason stepped back and took Haley from Cate so they could move quickly for the gate. Kevin and Ken followed, Gus followed last.

"Officers, arrest that woman. She is kidnapping our ward."

Jason glanced back. Two uniformed officers appeared at the front door. *What was going on here?*

Cate stopped and turned. "Kidnapping? Ward?"

"Keep moving, Cate, let Gus and the guys handle it."

But she didn't have time. With an agility Jason never anticipated, Harve was in front of Cate, shoving a pristine manila envelope at her. "This will prove our claim."

"Claim? You have no claim other than the fact that you are Haley's grandparents. You have no other claim on her as long as I'm her mother."

Jason handed Haley back to Cate, slipped the envelope out of her fingers and, using the light from the front door, quickly scanned the documents. "Impossible."

Gus and the twins surrounded Cate and Haley as the uniformed officers flanked their colleagues on the force.

"Move aside," Helene commanded her troops as she shouldered her way through to Cate.

Jason passed the documents to Kevin who quickly scanned them and shook his head. "You don't need the officers, Mrs. Malloy."

"Jace?" Cate's frightened voice burned loathing into his soul.

"They've been granted temporary ex-parte custody of Haley." Haley's grandparents were malicious, and he vowed from this moment to fight them with every ounce of his being.

"No. That's impossible!"

Helene placed a hand on Haley's shoulder.

Cate swatted it off.

Ken quickly stepped in between Helene and Cate. The uniformed officer next to Cate watched them closely.

Jason, about to object, noticed the scowl Ken directed at the Malloys, and realized Ken was protecting Cate from their possible accusation of assault. Something the Malloys must have planned on by having the HPD there.

"Mommy?" Haley started to cry.

"Harve, please take her in."

Cate held her daughter tighter.

Kevin give Cate a look of heartbreaking compassion. "Don't make this harder for your little girl. Now isn't the time." He gently took Haley, and gave her to her grandfather who moved swiftly toward the house.

"No, please. You can't take her."

Ken held Cate as she squirmed, desperate to run after her baby, her life.

Jason was impotent in the face of this treachery. Cate's world has just collapsed. He'd told her to believe and this parody of law was the result.

Haley, squirming in Harve's arms, dropped Hippity. "Mommy?" she cried.

Walking toward the house with imperial grace, Helene inclined her head as she passed them.

Rigid with fury, Jason tossed the orders in Helene's face. "I don't know how you were able to do this, but it won't stand."

"Of course it will. And you're better off to leave it alone."

"That will never happen."

"Your mistake."

"Jace!"

The agony in Cate's voice nearly broke him.

CATE LOOKED BLINDLY TOWARD THE INKY BLACK OF THE OCEAN AT the loneliest hour of the night as Gus drove them away from the Malloy estate.

Away from her baby. Now in the legal custody of the Malloys.

Impossible.

She'd wanted to fight them, use her fists, tear Haley away from their arms, just as they'd done to her. She wasn't the unfit mother, Helene Malloy was. Look what she'd done to Richard.

How was it possible for anyone to take this kind of life-altering legal action without a hearing or something that would have alerted her to what those slimy Malloys were up to?

Money and power would buy a lot of slime.

Tears wet her cheeks, but she didn't have the energy or will to wipe them away.

Jason had told Helene the orders wouldn't stand, but of course they would. What did she, broke and unemployed, have to battle the mighty Malloys with?

Nothing but a mother's love. And that wouldn't be enough. Not against this kind of power.

Jason had asked her to believe. Believe they'd find Haley and bring her home. And Cate had dared believe him. Now she realized that was foolish, only setting herself up for heartache.

"We're here ... Cate?"

Slowly swiveling her head toward Jason, she realized the car had stopped. "This isn't the charter terminal."

"No, why would it be? It's the Halekulani."

"We're not leaving?"

Jason slipped into the backseat, his lips close to her ear. "When did you ever run away from a fight? We're sure as hell not leaving. Don't give in to this—I'm not."

She looked into his eyes, where anger from the Malloy encounter still pulsed and burned, and she wanted it to burn in hers, too.

It wouldn't ignite.

The Malloys held all the cards; they were rich as Croesus, Haley was their granddaughter and the only heir to Richard's monumental trust.

And maybe, just maybe they were right, maybe she couldn't take care of her daughter. "I don't know, Jace, it seems pretty hopeless."

"You're not saying you'd rather leave Haley with the Malloys, are you? With people who don't care about her as child, but simply as a name, a symbol?"

She bent beneath his words, each one a body blow, clutching her stomach, rocking back and forth as sobs she couldn't control slipped through her lips.

"Sir? May I help you?" the parking valet asked, worry evident in his voice.

"No, we'll be fine," Jason assured the man, who only moved a few feet away and hovered. "Gus, I don't want to leave Cate. Would you go in and ask for Mr. Glenn, give him my card, ask for the Royal Suite, but I'll take the two-bedroom Halekulani if the Royal's not available. And hey, ask them to get me a car. A Mustang like yours would be perfect. Thanks. Oh, and, Gus, get me the best lawyer this town has."

"You got it, bro."

Jason was grateful Gus had the sense to raise the roof of the convertible before he left, giving Cate a small measure of privacy from the hotel's guests, for despite what he'd told the valet, he wasn't sure at all they'd be fine.

He reached over the front seat and grabbed Hippity, thankful he'd had the presence to pick up the bunny lying on the bricks where Haley had dropped him. He had no clue what Cate's reaction might be, but he hoped it might give her something to cling to, a life preserver of sorts.

She pressed the bunny against her heart. And broke his.

Her ravaged face, her haunted, swollen eyes, and the air of defeat surrounding her chided him. He'd been the one who told her to believe they'd simply pick up Haley and head home. And now, this woman in front of him, this Cate he'd once loved, was someone he'd never seen before.

Even at Mountain Hearth—God, was it only yesterday?— when she'd stood defiantly in front of him, asking for the truth and getting it, she'd been upset but not destroyed.

Not like this.

How could he make this better for her? *Nothing will be better until she has Haley. Then how can I get the fight back into her?*

"Ahem."

Jason looked over to find Gus standing by the car.

"Glenn was sorry the Royal was booked, but you've got the Halekulani and a car is coming. Didn't know you owned part of the hotel, bro."

"Not so much the hotel. It's owned by a real estate company in Japan. I own stock in the company."

"Whatever, they like you here. And when my niece gets

married, I'm gonna remember this and you." He winked, then turned serious. "Want help getting Cate upstairs?"

Jason wasn't sure if he needed help or not. Gently grasping Cate's face, he made her look at him. "Can you make it to the room?"

She nodded once.

He passed her bag to the hovering valet and held out his hand, ready to grab her if she faltered. She said she could do it, but she looked so damn fragile.

And she did. Her legs wobbled for an instant, then in pure Cate fashion, independent and intensely private, she donned her invisible cloak of observer, preferring that over being the subject of scrutiny herself, stood straight and walked, slowly but under her own power, into the hotel.

"I'll be back early in the morning," Gus said, his admiration for her evident as even he stood a bit a taller.

Cate had that effect on most people. The notable exception being the Malloys.

THE MINUTE THEY ENTERED THE SUITE'S SMALL FOYER, CATE deflated, leaning heavily against him. Jason steered her toward one of the bedrooms, where she collapsed on the bed, hugging Hippity tightly.

He pulled the comforter over her, closed the door and leaned against it, his mind whirling at the change of events. What the hell had happened? How could it have gone from a simple "let's go get Haley," to the Malloys now having temporary custody?

Scrubbing a weary hand across his face, he knew, despite what he'd told Cate, they had a major uphill battle on their hands. And he itched to start it. But it was close to midnight here, 4 a.m. Colorado time, he was beat, and there was nothing concrete he could wrap his mind around and work out, except the images of Haley, Cate, Harve and Helene, and the damned custody order.

Calling room service, he ordered a couple of legal pads, pens, several pots coffee and three breakfasts for 8 a.m. Cate would want coffee first, then food, if she wanted anything at all. And if not, he'd do his best to make sure she ate something. He knew she'd run herself into the ground and get sick if she didn't.

God, he knew her so well.

But if you really knew her, why did she leave you?

Frustrated that he allowed the question to creep into his mind, he was annoyed he allowed the memory of that night to resurface. And even more angry that if he were honest with himself, that the memory was never far from the surface, no matter how deep he tried to bury it.

That night, so many years ago, he'd turned the pool house into a white bower of flowers, fairy lights and candles. They'd fixed dinner together and eaten it on the patio, and then he'd led her into the little pool house, knowing she was expecting a tryst, as it was their favorite room for making love.

The flowers, lights and warm scent of candles delighted her, and she'd whirled around to find him on bended knee, two-carat Tiffany solitaire in hand.

And asked her to marry him.

The lights reflected in her eyes blurred with happy tears, and he knew she was going to grant him the gift of a lifetime. Then her eyes turned opaque when he mentioned he couldn't wait to start a family. A family neither of them ever had, but always wanted.

Without a word, she fled. Running out of there as if the furies themselves were after her.

Leaving him with ashes, then an anger so great it nearly ate him alive.

Now he was too exhausted to do anything but let the memory play until he could sleep.

So he stretched out on the couch, not wanting the second bedroom right now, and watched the lights from Waikiki play on the ceiling.

THE VIEW OF BEACH FROM THE SUITE'S LANAI NEVER CEASED TO please Jason. The looming crater of Diamond Head to the east, the spectrum of blues the ocean offered, the palm trees and the brightly garbed, or barely garbed, sun worshippers on the beach appealed to him nearly as much as the grand mountains of Colorado.

Today that wasn't the view he was seeing. Two blonde heads touching in reunion played out in front of his eyes for the umpteenth time, and he was already on his second cup of coffee in ten minutes.

The suite's doorbell chimed.

Gus stood at the door, a bakery box in hand. "How's Cate?"

"Asleep," Jason said quietly, leading the way out to the lanai.

"That's probably a good thing. That show the Malloys put on last night completely beat her up. By the way, I figure they knew we were coming."

"Yeah, Anders would have let them know."

"More than that, bro. It was night."

"So?"

"The gates were open and they had a couple of uniforms at the ready. The gates on those estates are never open unless they're expecting someone and especially if they thought a media circus might begin. Did you tell them when your flight was arriving?"

"No, Cate couldn't reach them at all. After Anders's call to them, they were ghosts."

"Didn't think so. And why wasn't Luci charged? It was all staged. All I do know for certain at this point is there're too many unanswered questions and I don't like it. I immediately put my guys back on duty. One in the front, one in the back."

"The back is the Pacific."

Gus snagged a piece of bacon off a plate. "And he's in a boat or walking the beach. Tough duty," he said, and chuckled. "But I want to make sure Haley is still there and okay. The Malloy show didn't only hurt Cate, you know."

"I know. I don't think I'll ever forget Haley's last cry for her mommy."

"Nor will I," Cate said.

Both men turned to see Cate standing in the middle of the suite, still looking fragile but not so haunted.

Jason pulled out a chair at the glass table. "You should eat, I have breakfast here."

"You're always feeding me."

"I know what works."

"Then coffee first, please."

Gus nodded toward the bakery box. "Macadamia nut and white chocolate muffins. Lelani made them for you, Cate."

"Lelani? 'ohana?"

Gus smiled as Jason poured her a cup of coffee. "My daughter."

Enough chit chat. Jason bit his tongue to hold back his urge to take charge, move this onward now and start fixing the problem. Instead he watched as Cate quickly drank the hotel's special Kona brew and poured another cup. He wasn't in charge, she was, but he and Gus were damn well going to help. Haley needed their help.

"Ready to talk strategy?" Gus asked her when she was on her second cup.

"If you think we should."

"Think we should?" Jason echoed. "That's pretty unenthusiastic, Cate."

"I guess I'm feeling pretty unenthusiastic. This is Hawai'i and they are the Malloys."

He set his coffee cup down hard, china ringing on the glass table. "And you're Haley's mother and I'm Jason St. Pierre, and I'll be damned if they think they can steal a child from her mother, without any consequences. This was planned and paid for. They're evil, Cate, but they will not beat us."

"Hey, don't forget Gus Tanaka in this trio of champions," Gus said, tilting his cup in Cate's direction. "So, first off, Jason, you asked for counsel, and I've lined up one of the island's best."

"And are we using 'ohana?" Jason asked.

"Almost family. Close enough to the wedding to count. Grant's law firm is very busy, but my second cousin told him now or never, so the wedding's on for the end of next month."

"Why counsel?" Cate asked.

"It's more than us finding out how the Malloys did this, it's who they used and how Luci was involved. That order was ex-parte, so that means it was done without your involvement. Why would a judge issue that and so quickly? It had to be done yesterday, a custody order can't be done without the child being in the state in which custody is being granted. And if it's a temporary order, Grant indicated there will be a final orders hearing. Attorneys like being in from the beginning. It's better for the case."

Jason watched Cate digest this latest news. She stared out over the exotic view, and he was sure she saw none of it. The hand holding the coffee cup began to tremble, and before she could spill any of the hot brew, he wrapped his hand around hers, gentling it.

"I'm sorry," she said, dashing away tears that spilled across her cheeks.

Jason hated the Malloys with a vehemence that choked him.

"I just can't believe I have to fight for the return of *my* daughter. That *I* have to regain custody. She's *my* daughter."

Cate walked to the railing, and Jason shared a quick glance with Gus, who knew as well as he did that this wasn't a slam dunk. He just didn't want Cate to know.

"What happens if this doesn't work?" she asked.

So much for that idea. "It will."

Cate silently filled in Jason's unspoken words: *believe that it will.*

She wasn't certain she dared believe in anything else again. And even as that thought crossed her mind, she relived Haley screaming "Mommy."

The only way she knew to tackle this was to use her rusty method of creating an op-ed piece. Get the facts, lay out the direction of the editorial and then dig in and make the piece work, make it unassailable. Those were the only strengths she had, and she was pretty sure they weren't enough, but then she had Jason, Gus and now this attorney, Grant.

She looked at Jason, then Gus, and nodded. "We can try," she said. Listening to her wimpy words echo in her ears, she didn't like them at all. She needed anger and that was easy to find. All she had to think of was her daughter's new bangs. How dare Helene do anything to Haley?

"Let me rephrase that, let's give the bastards hell. I want my daughter back."

9

CATE LAUGHED AT JASON'S STARTLED EXPRESSION. SHE *HAD* DONE A one-eighty attitude change as the liquid energy of adrenaline pushed aside her apathy, firing her up. She wasn't going to lose Haley without a war, not simply a battle.

If she looked in the mirror, she knew she'd see in her eyes the light of battle Jason had in his eyes last night, reflecting back, firing her up, moving her forward.

The unbelievable shock delivered last night was payback by the Malloys, and it had worked. Cate couldn't deny for the six months since Richard's death, she'd been stretched to the limit emotionally and physically, and then to have Haley missing and the Malloys' calculated and staged revenge pushed her almost to the dark brink of depression and apathy.

She loved the Hawaiian word 'ohana, for that was what she felt surrounding her. "Gus, can 'ohana mean extended family?"

"Yes, of course."

"Then let's get this 'ohana working."

"Stand, please," Gus requested.

She looked at him quizzically. Gus just motioned her up

with his thumb, and so she stood, to suddenly be enveloped in a bear hug.

Hugging Gus back was good and right, and she laughed with a full heart as Gus hugged Jason and he actually returned the hug.

Then Jason wrapped his arms around her. "Good call, Cate," he whispered into her hair. She held him tight for a moment, then reluctantly let go, sat down again and got to work.

"Gus, what are the chances of finding Luci and Mark? I want to see their faces when I show up. I'm betting nobody expected me to come to Hawai'i , at least not this quickly," she said, then mouthed a thank you to Jason.

From the start, it was he who made everything work, allowing her to follow the path Luci laid, all the way to Hawai'i .

Jason rewarded her with a stomach-melting smile, this one reaching his eyes. For the second time since this whole nightmare started, the smile wasn't social or perfunctory. It was all for her.

"Mark was easy to find. He's staying at the main competitor's hotel, the Bayan Bay," Gus reported. "The underwater war games continue through tomorrow, and lucky for us, the staging area is about five minutes away at the Kewalo Basin Harbor. It's a multi-tank dive, but I'm betting they'll be up no later than five this afternoon. If Mark does well tomorrow, he's in the final battle, which takes place at Kauai over the weekend."

"And Luci is with him?"

"No. At least not registered at that hotel. We're canvassing in a radius from there."

Cate churned over this news. Why wouldn't Luci be with Mark? Obviously they were in love, and born from that a deceitful pact had been formed. "I think we should find Luci and talk to her first."

"Because?" Jason asked.

"I think she brought him onboard with this. I think she was the major player." She looked apologetically at Jason. "I'm sorry, I know we're talking about your people."

"No longer my people. I wonder how I missed this ... twice."

Gus's phone buzzed and he simply punched it on, no greeting. Cate listened to his side of the conversation.

"Just the car? Okay, yes, and let me know immediately, boat or plane, yeah, it'll be a charter for sure." After disconnecting the call, he met Cate's gaze. "The Malloys left the estate in a chauffeured town car. My guy is on them."

"You mentioned boat or plane, do you think they're going to leave the island, head to their ranch?"

Gus didn't have the chance to answer before his phone buzzed again, twice. "Got it. Good." He punched a button then listened for a second, his lips curving in a mischievous grin. "Good, stay put, but move if they move."

"Haley is still at the compound, walking the beach with a big Hawaiian woman—"

"Emme, been with the family forever," Jason said.

Cate whirled around. "Thank God. I couldn't bear for her to be jerked around in an effort to hide from me."

Jason gently took the cup away and pointed to the cart sitting next to the table. "Food. Dig in, I know you're starving."

The sweet, tangy smell of the freshly cut pineapple was too much to resist, so she didn't. It melted in her mouth. The bacon was still warm, and she added one of Leilee's muffins to her plate.

All conversation stopped as she ate ravenously at first, then slowed and actually savored each bite. "You got another call?" she asked Gus, who just pocketed his phone for the third time.

"Yup. We found Luci. She's in a time-share at the Ilikai with her mother. Still want a go at her first?"

Cate nodded and put down her fork.

"We'll take my car. I need to stop by the office first and get a few things," Gus said.

"Give me a minute?" Cate asked, not waiting for the answer. She ran into the bedroom, rummaged through her bag, and tossed on a sundress she'd packed on a whim. After running her fingers through her hair and a washcloth over her face, she was ready to face Luci and hoped she didn't slap the traitorous bitch.

GUS'S OFFICE WAS IN A DOWNTOWN HIGH-RISE WITH UNDERGROUND parking. They took the elevator to the penthouse.

"No one to hear the screams when we interrogate," he said with a laugh.

Cate wasn't at all sure he was kidding.

The office suite was decorated simply, but she knew the receptionist's desk was made from curly koa wood, and expensive. Before she'd sold it, a similar one had graced Richard's home office.

There were six doors off the main entry. Gus led them to the last door, his office, with another massive Ka desk dominating the room, and a view through floor-to-ceiling windows of both Diamond Head and Waikiki.

He slipped into a locked room and came back wearing shorts and a T-shirt with "Hang Loose" printed on it, along with a ratty yet compact backpack.

"Going native?" Jason asked.

"Blending, bro," Gus said, throwing him a set of surf shorts and another T-shirt. "You can't wear khakis on the beach, you'll get the *why* quick enough. Bathroom's through there." Gus nodded to a door hidden in the paneling. Jason went in, changed and was out in under a minute, his clothes rolled up and tucked under his arm, shoes dangling from his fingers.

"No flip flops?"

"Ran out of your size."

"Now all you need is a boogie board," Cate said, smiling at the picture he presented, completely at ease in his shorts and shirt, barefoot and tan from the Colorado summer sun. He still commanded attention, but seemed more approachable, and ... oh, dear God ... sexy. A bit of stubble, more than a five o'clock shadow, graced his face. He hadn't shaved this morning and his hair was mussed from pulling on the shirt.

She wanted to touch his hair, muss it up more, and recall how it felt between her fingers—

"Earth to Cate!"

She felt a nudge on her shoulder, stopped daydreaming and refocused on Jason who nodded toward Gus, and realized he'd been trying to get her attention. Warm embarrassment crept up her cheeks.

"Hold out your wrist, please."

She did as asked, trying to ignore the knowing twinkle in Gus's brown eyes as he clasped a delicate silver charm bracelet around her right wrist.

"Here's how we're going to work it. Luci seems pretty sure of herself. She's not hiding or running. The hibiscus charm is a microphone, and it'll transmit to me. See what you can get her to admit. Let's give it a try." Gus ducked back into that mysterious room and closed the door.

Cate tried to act normal and not do anything that would make the bracelet look conspicuous. The gleam in Jason's eyes told her he knew exactly what she was doing.

"If I start fidgeting with it, do something," Cate pleaded.

"I'll think of something."

"And if I look like I might slap her, stop me. Promise?"

"No promises," Jason said with a chuckle.

Gus came back into the room. "Perfect. Let's go." He led

them out of the suite and locked the door. "And, uh, Cate, when you get to her, don't slap her, 'k?"

"Can't promise, but I'll try to restrain myself."

GUS PARKED AT THE FAR END OF THE MARINA NEAR THE HILTON lagoon. The Ilikai was diagonally situated across the street, but the beach was only footsteps away.

Checking in with his guys, Gus reported Luci was sunbathing, wearing a red maillot and a big floppy sunhat about 200 yards down from the marina, beach side of the lagoon. "Give me a couple of minutes to move down the beach, then do your thing."

Jason eyed Cate. She blended perfectly in her bright yellow sundress, and he was grateful Gus made him change. It would have been hard to wrest any information from Luci if he was still dressed like her boss.

Cate radiated an energy he hadn't seen in years. For the parties, and openings, the social rounds they'd both been obligated to attend, she looked and dressed the part. And she'd had the socially accepted ennui down pat.

But now she had a fight in her and, for want of a better description, she burned from the inside. She whirled around, cupped his cheek and kissed him, then fumbled for his hand and pulled him along onto the beach.

The fleeting warmth of her kiss stunned him, thrilled him, and he wished the warmth of her lips lingered. Memories once fueled by anger were replaced by this new moment of energy and shared task at hand. She had pegged it, they were 'ohana while they fought to get Haley back.

The sand felt good between his toes, and despite the urgency of finding Luci and starting their investigation, he took a moment and steered her closer to the foamy tide, letting it play over their feet, tickling. Her laughter was clear; his felt clean, reborn.

"I see her," she whispered, though there was no need. The beach was noisy with life.

Cate gripped his hand tighter as she headed directly for Luci, sunning on a tatami mat, accompanied by an older woman sitting in a canvas beach chair.

When they got closer, he let go of her hand and hung back, giving Cate the surprise factor.

Planting herself between the sun and Luci, she got both ladies' attention. Big white sunglasses hid Luci's eyes, but her mouth tightened with shock.

When he decided it was time to make his presence known, it amused him that Luci actually scooted back a bit on her blanket.

"Jason, this is a surprise. Mother, I'd like to introduce you to my employer, Jason St. Pierre."

Interesting game Luci was playing. "Former employer, Mrs. Roth. Former."

Luci cocked her head to the side and pulled back her wide-brimmed hat. "Why is that?"

"Let's start with kidnapping. Why the hell aren't you in jail?" he asked.

She stood and, with great aplomb, wrapped a vivid red sarong around herself, all the while keeping her gaze glued on Cate. "Mother, would you mind terribly giving us a bit of space? Maybe grab us all some fresh papaya from the ABC store across the road?"

"No, I think I'd rather listen to this. There is nothing you can do to Luci, Mr. St. Pierre. It was all legal."

"Legal?" Cate said, her voice soft.

Jason knew exactly what that tone meant; this was going to be fascinating.

"Just how is this legal? Stealing my daughter, taking her across state lines? Kidnapping isn't legal in the U.S. of A." Cate crossed her arms, and only Jason was aware of how careful she was to make sure the bracelet was on top, fully in view, to record each word as Cate led Luci down the path.

Luci stretched, giving the impression of complete boredom, and Jason had to admit she put on a good show. "Steal? I didn't steal or kidnap or whatever other dramatic words you choose to use. Don't you remember us talking about taking Haley to her grandparents for a vacation? Remember how excited she was by the luau birthday party?"

Cate stood stock still. "That was simply talk. I'd made no plans."

"Haley believes you did. And so did the Malloys when I told them."

"How did you get her things packed? Convince her to go with *you*?"

"Hmm, let's see ... do you recall the interview Friday, at the *Los Angeles Star*?"

"There was no interview. It was a totally wasted trip, but I was gone. Lucky for you, wasn't it?"

Wasted trip? That's what she said to Anders. Jason had to get to the bottom of this.

Luci's little shrug was elegant at the same time it was despicable. "Believe me when I say the Malloys have it all sewn up. You lose."

Luci took off her sunglasses, Jason was shocked at the bitterness in her eyes and was instantly on higher alert. Even Cate took a step back from the venom directed their way.

He noticed the charm bracelet had slipped, the hibiscus

charm faced the ocean now, not Luci. He nudged Cate's elbow and she turned to look at him. He glanced at the bracelet and back at her in a millisecond, but even worked up, she got the message and re-crossed her arms, charm unobstructed.

"The evidence was so compelling, the judge signed the temp order with a flourish. Too bad it was only a temporary order. I think it was the kitchen fire video that turned the tide. Remember? It was a good thing I was cooking with Haley that day. She could have been burned, or ... worse." Luci sighed. "Another sad note on the long list of inadequate parental care."

"Oh my God, you started that fire? Are you out of your mind? You could have seriously hurt her!" Cate balled her fists and instantly Jason put his hand on her back, unsure whether she would really punch her or not. He sure as hell itched to.

"A couple of pieces of dried bread on fire weren't going to hurt Haley, but on film it looked much worse, and that hurt you."

"Why would you want to hurt us? I thought you loved Haley. You said you did."

"You're not listening. It's not us, it's you." She poked a finger into Cate's chest.

Jason swatted Luci's hand away.

Instantly Mrs. Roth stood, moving to stand next to her daughter.

An odd face-off formed.

"And people like you, Jason." Luci practically spat the words at him. "You both use people, but for the moment, let's stay on you, Cate. You dumped Jason for the better man. Then realizing you were stuck with a child and a husband, and your precious Pulitzer was only gathering dust, you started making demands. You were unhappy, and when Richard couldn't make you happy, he tried buying your happiness, but that didn't work. You were bored by him, by the lifestyle, but you wouldn't let him go. Haley was your meal ticket."

Luci vibrated with rage. How was it possible Jason had never seen this side of her?

"And then you simply killed him."

10

LUCI'S ACCUSATION RANG IN CATE'S EARS.

There was no truth in her words, but Cate still harbored guilt from that hideous day. She and Richard *had* fought the night before his climb, and she knew he'd been struggling with something big the last few months. In addition, his partnership with Jason was on the rocks, but that hadn't seemed to bother him much.

She begged him for answers, had even called him irresponsible for thinking of climbing when not in top mental condition, but she hadn't killed him.

"He died on Longs Peak. It was an accident. A sad, needless tragedy."

Luci's hand was up so fast that Cate felt the hot sting of her slap on her cheek before she could dodge the blow.

Instantly, Jason grabbed Luci's arm, spinning her away so fast she stumbled and fell on her beach mat.

Luci scrambled up, and Mrs. Roth gripped her shoulder, holding her back. "Steady, honey, steady."

"You ruined him—he died up on that stupid mountain because he couldn't concentrate. You took him from me."

Cate fought putting her hand on her cheek to sooth the sting. She wouldn't give Luci the satisfaction. "Took him from you? What are you talking about?"

"You didn't know because we didn't want you to know. D.I.V.O.R.C.E," Luci spelled out, yelling as loud as she could, getting the attention of everyone on the beach who was within hearing. A fair number stopped and stared.

Cate didn't know where to look. She couldn't look at Jason, didn't want to see what was on his face, couldn't look again at the victorious expression on Luci's face, because she was afraid she'd deck her, claw her eyes out, then spit on her.

Instead, she took a deep breath, realizing the only thing she could do was press on.

"Does Mark know you don't—and never did—love him?"

"Mark was simply a tool."

Cate prayed Gus was getting this, and hoped Mark would crack and spill the rest when he heard the voice of his beloved trashing their relationship.

"I've loved two men in my life, my father and Richard, and they're both gone," Luci cried. "Because of rich, unfeeling bottom feeders like you, Jason, and bitches who take and take and take like you, Cate. The Malloys can't have Richard, but they can have Haley. I can't have Richard, but I have enough money now to take care of Mom.

"And you, Cate? You'll never have Haley. You threw away Jason and killed Richard. Haley's better off without you. Her money is safe, you can't destroy her with your incessant need. She'll get over you, go to the best schools and carry on the Malloy tradition of greatness."

Cate wanted to argue, but there was nothing she could say that would change Luci's delusions.

Pride stiffened her back as she took Jason's arm. "I think we're done here."

Turning her back on Luci and her mother, she measured her steps, not allowing them to see any emotion as she and Jason walked away.

"He loved me, the three of us were going to be the real family he so wanted," Luci yelled after them on a sob.

JASON WAITED BY GUS'S CAR, WATCHING CATE PACE THE PARKING lot.

Luci had delivered salvo after salvo of shock-and-awe revelations. He'd worked beside her for over six years and never had an inkling of the resentment that ate at her, destroying her soul, leaving only the bitter need to hurt another person as she herself hurt.

Luci apparently wanted to not only hurt but potentially destroy that person.

Yet Cate wasn't destroyed, she was angry. Fuming mad, ready to take on anyone. Watch out, Mark Adams.

Jason wondered what it said about him, that he hadn't recognized two of his people working behind his back, lying, cheating, and scheming, for he was sure, even without interviewing the man, that Mark was as guilty as Luci.

Gus jogged up and nodded toward Cate at the end of the parking row. "Working off her anger," Jason explained, just as she turned around and saw them.

"Gus, did you get it all?" she called, running back.

"If you ever want to change professions, you come work for me. You got her riled up enough to admit her relationship with Richard, and got her to admit more than I dreamed. Good job. How are you holding up?"

"Mad as hell, frankly."

Gus chuckled and checked his watch. "Mark's dive probably

isn't over yet, and I need to get this to the office and put it on a disc and into the safe, then do a bit more digging. Can you wait until tomorrow to tackle him?"

"No, but I will if I have to. Before his dive or after?"

"Before," Jason and Gus simultaneously answered.

"And I'm keeping a couple of men on him," Gus added. "I'm not sure Luci would contact him, she seemed quite indifferent about the dude, but just in case."

"And I don't care if we rattle him enough that he misses the competition," Jason said, earning a vigorous nod from Cate.

"Do you want the bracelet back now?" she asked.

"Yeah, just to check the battery. Don't want to lose a bit of tomorrow's confrontation."

Cate danced like a boxer, fists up, jabbing and then faking an upper cut. "Yup, me neither." Then she lowered her arms and unclasped the bracelet, handing it to Gus.

"Instead of Gus dropping us off at the hotel, do you want to walk back?" Jason asked, laughing at her energy. "Gus says it's less than a half-hour walk, or as wound up as you are, fifteen minutes."

Her smile was worth the blisters he'd get walking that distance barefoot. He couldn't put on his wrinkled clothes and wouldn't wear his street shoes with the surfer shorts. He did have some pride.

Gus slipped into his car and handed Jason his bundle of clothes. "Go through the Hilton Village grounds until you find Kalia Road, then follow it to the Halekulani. Meet you at the Basin around eight tomorrow." He waved and drove off.

The smile dropped from Cate's face the moment Gus left. This was more the mood Jason had expected after the Luci encounter. "Still want to walk back?"

"Yeah, I'm tired of planes and cars and chasing." She glanced up, her eyes filled with guilt. "Damn, I'm sorry. Without you, I couldn't have done any of this."

"It's okay, I know what you mean. What you want most is to cuddle with Haley. To hunker down. To be done with this insanity."

She nodded and reached out her hand.

First she'd kissed him, now she reached out for him?

Not sure she realized the implications of her actions, and not willing to add any more to her load by rejecting her, even if it was for his own sanity, he clasped her hand in his, and realized as he had with the kiss, that it felt right. And the bitter memories dimmed just a bit more.

They started down the sidewalk out of the marina. "Hey, there's the ABC store Luci wanted her mom to disappear into. Come on, I need flip-flops." He kept a tight grip on her hand as they darted across the street, dodging traffic, and ran into the store. He picked out sandals and a couple of Cokes as Cate wandered the store. "See anything you like?"

She held up a cute T-shirt of a blonde little surfer girl on a board. Leani, an Aloha Honey Girl, complete with lei and hula skirt. "This would be Haley, always on or in the water."

Jason added the shirt to the pile.

"No, I didn't mean for you to buy it. It's just cute."

"She can wear it when you two play on the beach."

Tears shimmered in her eyes, and she looked down at the small, folded shirt as the clerk put in it the sack. Jason paid the bill and slipped on his flip-flops.

"Much better," he said with an exaggerated sigh, hoping to make her laugh.

It worked. This time he grabbed her hand and they zigzagged their way through the Hilton's grounds and up Kalia Road, drinking their Cokes, strolling along.

"Aloha, Mr. St. Pierre," the Halekulani's concierge greeted as they entered the hotel lobby, earning a raised brow from Cate.

"Long story, I'll tell you later. Room service, hotel restaurant or someplace else?"

She looked down at her clothes and pointed at him in his board shorts. "Room service."

"Right. Do you want to go shopping for some clothes? This trip may take a bit longer than expected." He winced as the words left his lips, but it was the truth. This was far more complicated than simply picking up Haley and going home.

"No. Thanks though, I really don't feel up to it. It feels like something I don't want to devote energy to."

Jason nodded, completely understanding her lack of enthusiasm for anything other than the task at hand. A daunting, life-changing task.

But they'd made headway today. Cate bravely took the brunt of the confrontation with Luci.

Face-to-face confrontation wasn't her style. He well knew she'd prefer to be alone and solve this problem through studying the court documents, fitting the pieces together. Research and observation were her modus operandi. But that wasn't the way this fight was going to play out.

"You know what I would like, if it's possible?" Cate asked. "A glass of wine on the lanai before dinner comes up."

"Sounds perfect. Chateauneuf-du-Pape Blanc, right?"

How did Jason remember this? Cate would have sworn, as angry as he was at first after she'd left him, then as icily distant as he'd been the past six years, any intimate detail like this would be wiped from his memory.

While she'd never stopped remembering.

Which was one of the things that eventually angered Richard into making the second major shift in their relationship.

Richard had always known the second she "left" him, lost in a memory of Jason. She'd never been aware of her facial changes, the way her eyes became soft, unfocused and—according to Richard—a tiny smile lifted her lips. Until, in a fit of anger, he accused her of still loving Jason. He turned her to a mirror, told her to look at herself closely, then left the room, slamming the door.

After that he'd had another king bed moved into their room, telling her the only reason he was sharing a room at all was because he didn't want Haley to think anything was wrong between them. She was too young to get the significance of two beds, but not too young to understand their antagonism, which he vowed never to let show in front of her.

A vow Cate concurred with. And heaven knows the room was big enough. She would climb into Richard's bed for a "family" snuggle if Haley came in frightened by a nightmare or just to wake them up.

And to give her husband credit, he kept that vow until his death, making sure Haley never witnessed the truth of their marriage. Nor did he tell her the truth of her birth.

If everything Luci had said was true, Cate wondered how Richard was going to explain a divorce to Haley.

And Cate wondered again if he'd ever loved her or was it only the picture of the family they presented that he loved.

Pieces fell into place with sudden clarity.

That night, before the climb, she'd mentioned she was going to start writing again, that since Haley was going to start kindergarten in the fall, it was time for her to find something additional to look forward to, something additional to do. He had his climbing and his business.

He looked at her, walked to the door and carefully shut it. He'd asked why Haley wasn't enough, to which she'd replied Haley was the love of her life, but she needed these other things to be happy, that sitting down at a desk and writing was something she had looked forward to each day, and that was missing from her life.

Richard had looked at her, then erupted in anger saying he'd wanted her to fill his life, but obviously that had been a joke, a sad joke on him learned only after Haley had been born. He'd also said that she should go ahead and find her own life, but his was always going to require Haley in it, so get used to it. That night he'd slept in the guest room. He'd left for his climb before Cate rose the next morning.

He'd meant he was leaving her.

Jason interrupted her chaotic thoughts. "Wine is ordered and already on its way."

There was nothing she could do to change any of it. Richard's death, as she'd told Luci, was a horrible tragedy for all of them. Cate didn't despise her late husband, but his parents were on her list.

Jason's gaze questioned her silence.

She shook her head. "I was just replaying Richard's last conversation with me. He was telling me in so many words that he was leaving."

"And, how do you feel?"

"Sad that he never had the chance to find what he was looking for, accepting that it wasn't me, and still furious at the treachery that followed."

"I'M STUFFED AND TIRED, BUT I NEED A WALK. WANT TO COME with me?" Cate asked Jason as she pushed away her dessert plate, leaving only crumbs of the hotel's famed coconut cream cake.

"Sure. Absolutely. I need to walk some more."

Cate looked at him askance. "Yeah, I can tell you're totally into walking on Waikiki, in the moonlight, with ..." *me.*

Jason looked at her, his expression unfathomable, but she didn't read anger, mistrust or any of the myriad of other objectionable emotions she'd seen on his face over the past six years.

Then he shifted, his crooked smile catching her off guard. "Seriously, I can't put Band-Aids between my toes and that's where the blisters are, so if we walk, it will have to be barefoot, for both of us."

"The only way to walk on a beach. Let's go."

Laughter bubbled up as they slipped through the lobby like teens sneaking out for the night, sure that going barefoot through the elegant lobby wasn't something the Halekulani encouraged.

They passed the lit pool, its mosaic orchid shimmering under the water, and found the beach access. The sand was still warm beneath her feet, and Jason held her hand. Simple pleasures. It seemed like ages since she'd felt this way, and if Haley were skipping between them, it would have been perfect.

"I hate to break the mood, but I'd like to ask you a couple of questions about your interview at the *LA Star*."

"You mean my non-existent, wild-goose-chase interview."

"You did have an interview with Dickerson—that's what I don't understand."

Cate stopped at the edge of the water, only half registering the bubbles of foam as the tide rolled over her toes. "What do you mean I had an interview? How would you know?"

"I bought Richard's stake in the paper."

"Richard owned that paper?"

"Thirty percent. I had twenty-two percent. I started the process of buying his shares before his death, and the deal cleared all the hurdles a few weeks ago. Richard didn't understand why I wanted them, especially since the paper was losing money and readership."

Cate nodded, well aware that in the six years she'd been out of the business, the industry had changed. To the masses, the papers were dinosaurs. She'd wondered countless times how kids Haley's age were going to get responsible reporting on current events and not turn into mouthpieces for whichever agenda got to them first.

That's why she had loved writing op-ed pieces. Done right, an opinion offered a perspective, not a rant.

"So how did my interview play into this?"

"Dickerson wanted the *Star* to live, and I think news is still important, objective reporting vital. We have plans for moving the paper to strictly an online daily newspaper with a weekly recap on the weekends. Dickerson wanted "star" power to boost readership and asked my opinion on top op-ed writers. He didn't want the standard major players now in the game, whom he thinks of as basically propaganda puppets. He wanted someone people trusted. I recommended you.

"He didn't realize you were still in the game. I told him to ask. Simple."

Simple? It had been a godsend to get that phone call for an interview. She'd targeted the paper, sending in her resume months before, but had heard nothing back. And if she got the job, she and Haley could stay in Denver, since everything was done digitally now.

"But Dickerson wasn't there," Cate said. "He was on some retreat he takes annually and nobody knew anything about the interview. Even his secretary was gone. It was a total bust."

Worse than a bust, it had been humiliating.

"He annually takes off the last two weeks of August for fishing, has for thirty years and goes without any communication except for an emergency satellite phone," Jason said. "Not even his family goes. They're usually at their Seattle vacation cabin."

"Well, this interview was scheduled for the middle of his retreat. A total screw-up. And a pretty important one for me."

"Wait, think. Who said it had to be last Friday?"

Cate thought back, trying to marshal her thoughts. So much had happened it felt like weeks ago, not less than seven days. "The phone call came the week before last from Dickerson's secretary, offering the interview, and I told her I was honored and indicated that generally Fridays were my best day, because of Haley."

She glanced at Jason, needing to bring him into her life, explain her reason for being so rigid since she needed a job so badly, instead of being flexible about the interview day. "I wouldn't have been gone long, but Haley and I would have the weekend together to make up for her being with a babysitter. I spoil her I know, but after Richard ..." She trailed off.

"I don't think that's spoiling her, Cate. I think it's putting her first."

A warm moment of pleasure stole over her that they would agree on something so important to her as her daughter. "Anyway, she said she'd set up the date. Then a ticket comes via Fed-Ex on Thursday. Luci was there..."

Cate looked at Jason as another piece of this nasty puzzle began to fall into place. "Luci was there watching Haley as I was finishing the packing for the move. She was excited about my interview and came over early Friday morning so I could catch the flight.

"When I arrived, nobody at the Star knew anything. In fact the receptionist was almost rude about it. He actually filed his nails while telling me Dickerson wasn't there. When I refused to accept his answer and stormed back to the newsroom to check for myself, I realized he was right. An editor's desk is never neat as a pin. Dickerson's was. My only choice was to come home and take that 'stupid job,' as you called it."

Jason kicked at some foam, then met Cate's steady gaze. "I'm sorry I said that. I didn't realize things were so financially tough. They shouldn't have been. Who was the receptionist at the Star?"

"Robert B." She'd never forget the pompous twit who sneered as he told her she'd better hurry to catch her flight home as she couldn't afford to buy another ticket, then sashayed off, waving his left hand in the air, while she stood in the news room, defeated and confused. "He wore a purple suit, had blond spikey hair and has better skin than me. And for some weird reason, he seemed to know my financial situation."

Jason pulled out his phone and ran through his contacts list. "She's gonna hate me," he mumbled as he waited for connection. "Susan? St. Pierre here. Listen ..."

Cate moved up the beach to sit on the edge of one of the beached outrigger canoes. Her stomach burned, the pain radiated into her heart as she realized the extent the Malloys or Luci or both along with Mark had gone to in orchestrating the taking of her child. She'd never been the victim of such hateful actions.

She knew, at least in her eyes, her marriage had been a sham from day one, but she stuck with it because of Haley. To tear her away from her daddy wasn't an option, *but apparently tearing her away from her mommy was for Richard.*

She turned to watch the man she *did* love, pacing the beach in the moonlight as he worked his magic.

People in power often commanded respect, but Jason always earned it. He might ask for a favor as he was apparently doing now, but he would return it tenfold when needed.

He was also intensely focused once his mind was made up. A trait she admired until it was focused on her. He knew what was right, would take control and make it work. Even when the person might not agree on what the right direction would be.

And at that time, she couldn't handle the thought of having a child. It scared her silly. She'd never had the role model of a parent, only the endless gray of the foster system. And of course as an adult she understood that not all foster homes were as uncaring as the ones she'd suffered in, and many of the kids had been adopted into loving families. Nevertheless, it was what *she'd* experienced that created her fear of parenthood. She didn't want to be a parent like the ones who'd borne her, then abandoned her.

Cate pushed the past aside, for it was just that, the past. She'd learned, but too late, and now she and Jason had no future, at least the kind she wanted. But they had now, and she'd take the little bit of him she could get and hold that close to her heart.

Jason headed her way. She could tell by his gait the phone call yielded more unpleasant news.

"Susan pulled some strings; Robert Beauchamp quit the paper that same day, telling folks he was opening a beach bar in Cabo. Apparently everyone was surprised as the man never had money at the end of the month. And Dickerson's secretary did set up an interview for you, for the following Friday, and as usual practice, gave the Fed-Ex envelope to Robert to send out. This was set up."

"And I told Luci everything," Cate said. "She was always available when I needed to talk, like a confidante. God, how could I be so stupid, so gullible, so naïve. And if Richard needed the money so badly he was selling Star stock to you, he and Luci must have talked about this, and she'd have had some inside info on whom to approach—"

"Cate, you keep saying this, but Richard didn't need money."

———

11

JASON SAT NEXT TO HER ON THE OUTRIGGER CANOE. "DON'T LOOK at me as if I'm crazy, Richard didn't need money."

"What do you mean? I got the bills after he died and was blown away by the amounts owed. Richard always took care of the finances, the checking account was down to practically nothing, and the savings account the same, I was stunned." Cate said. "The brokerage accounts were Pay on Death for Haley. I sure as hell wasn't going to touch any of that."

"None of that makes sense—"

"Except that now I know Richard was planning on a divorce," she said slowly as she stared at the ocean. "I think he was already moving accounts. He was planning a new life. He didn't expect to die."

Jason saw the change in her immediately. Her shoulders dropped, her eyes closed, and then tears glistened on her cheeks. He gathered her close. They'd always fit together so well, like yin and yang. Nothing had changed that. He closed his eyes and let the rightness of holding her just be. He didn't fight to remain angry, he didn't resurrect the pain as a shield to keep her at arm's length.

He just held her.

"It was all so stupid, so remarkably stupid, you'd have thought we could have found a way to separate amicably, but if he loved Luci, he'd listen to her, and she hated me—"

He didn't want to hear any more about Richard, about this. Covering her mouth with his own stopped the words and exposed the need he'd been burying for years.

A sob escaped Cate's lips, and he swallowed it, not breaking their kiss.

In response, her arms wrapped around him, tightened, bringing him impossibly closer. Then her kiss changed, became demanding. Her fingers curled in his hair, holding his head still as she took control, nipping his bottom lip, bringing him closer still, as if to meld them together.

Something his body craved, his soul feared and his heart rejected. Even so he pressed her harder to him. "Cat," he murmured.

Her heat radiated through the thin sundress, clouding his mind further, firing his blood. He was aching hard and wanted her now. Hell, he'd wanted this for years, been haunted by the memory of their kisses. He wanted to sweep her up, carry her through the lobby—the hell with protocol—and lay her on the huge bed.

He wanted to hear her moan his name softly with passion, to feel her clench around him as pleasure rocked her. To feel his release into her. He wanted Cat and knew why.

Because in spite of her betrayal, she was everything joyful you weren't. She completed you, expanded you, created a world outside of computers, finances and deal making. Cat brought you to life.

Hawaiian slack-key music from one of the hotels drifted around them. He pulled away, only a few millimeters, but he needed to rein himself in. She slowly opened her eyes, questioning him and maybe herself.

"Dance with me, Cat." He held out his arms.

A smile curved her lips, and she fitted one hand into his, the other on his shoulder.

He moved slowly, right foot right, left foot to its side, left foot back, as Cate followed, waltzing on the sand. The beat wasn't right, but everything else was: the moonlight casting a beam across the ocean right to them. The shadow of the palm trees slightly hiding them from other moonlight strollers, and the heady scent of flowers mingling with the scent of Cate.

The music ended, and an elderly couple near the water applauded them.

Cate's laughter tinkled like an old Japanese glass wind chime and she curtsied. The couple waved and continued on.

He hadn't had moments like these since she'd left. He dated, wined and dined some of the most beautiful women in the world. He slept with many, but moments of fun like this, passion and completeness had escaped him. Maybe it was his fault, maybe he didn't want to feel it. *No, it wasn't the same, and you wanted Cate. Then you stopped trying to find anyone to take her place.*

"And don't start again," he mumbled to himself.

"Start what? Dancing?" Cate asked.

"No, just thinking out loud." *Lame answer, doofus.* He hoped she wouldn't dig further, because she could always tell when he lied. He didn't have her eye twitch, but she knew, regardless.

He braved her searching look and apparently satisfied her.

"Okay. Well, it's late." She knew he was hiding something. Neutral voice, bland comment.

"And it's been a long day," he agreed.

"Will you set a wake-up call?" she asked over her shoulder, already walking toward the hotel.

He didn't want the moment to end like this. Jogging the few steps to catch up with her, he grabbed her hand, holding tightly as she tried to pull it away. "I told you, it was nothing. A non-thought."

They entered the lobby, this time not worrying about bare feet. Despite what he'd said, the moment was changed, and they were back in reality, the moonlit magic of the beach behind them.

"I need a few things from the gift shop. Want anything?" he asked.

"Nope, I'm fine. Goodnight, Jason. And don't forget to wake me up in time for coffee."

Waiting until she was in the elevator, he headed to the hotel boutique. They both needed clothes, and if she didn't want to shop—he couldn't blame her for not wanting to—then he would. Passing the jewelry store, he spied the most perfect set of golden South Sea pearls and stared at them as so many things came into focus after that soul-searing kiss on the beach.

Like admitting wholly and without anger that he'd never stopped thinking about her.

If at a party, one he knew Richard and Cate were attending, he realized he'd unconsciously looked for her. And once she'd entered the room, he'd find her, stealing small glances. She played the room well, but there was always a sadness surrounding her he didn't understand. And when he saw her running down the road only days ago, arms waving, frantic about something, his heart knew he'd follow her to see if he could help.

He glanced back at the pearls in the window. They'd be perfect for Cate, yet he passed on by, knowing she'd say she'd never have a chance to wear them.

Too wound up to sleep, Cate opened the blackout curtains in the room and let the colors of a Honolulu night play in the room. She heard Jason come into the suite, a few noises as he moved around, then silence.

It was too quiet.

She opened the lanai door, hoping the sound of the surf would soothe her enough to sleep, but too many images and voices played through her head.

Was it only twenty-four hours ago that she'd arrived here, found, then lost her daughter? The image of Haley with a new haircut and wearing yellow pj's, crying for her mommy, wouldn't leave her brain. And the fear that she might not regain custody alternately froze her heart and fueled her anger red hot.

Sleep was useless. Cate stepped out to the lanai and watched the phosphorous waves break on the shore. Turning back to her room, she realized the door to Jason's bedroom was open as well.

Heart beating wildly, she stood to the side of his door and peeked in.

A shaft of moonlight lit the bed. The silvery whiteness of the sheet contrasted starkly with the bronzed sheen of his body. He was turned slightly from the door, so she felt safe to gaze, filling her mind with images to last a lifetime.

He'd slept nude when they were together and apparently still did. The sheet draped just across his hips. His shoulders and chest seemed broader, stronger, and she remembered he'd taken up running. And apparently lifting as well.

She itched to run her palm lightly over his chest, feel his muscles ripple under her touch as they once did.

He turned slightly, and she stepped back, deeper into the shadow of the lanai.

Listening intently, she heard nothing more and peeked around again. The sheet had drifted lower on his hips.

Her gaze drifted downward and then up to his face.

His eyes gleamed. Jason was awake.

Cate turned and took two hasty steps, then heard his voice. "Couldn't sleep?"

She was already caught, but debated answering. Her throat felt thick, from remembered passion ... and current hungers. "No," she whispered.

"Want me to rub your back?"

No, that always led to things other than sleep. "Yes."

He patted the spot beside him. Cate took a deep breath, knowing if she took one step forward, that step was taking her over the edge with no safety net below. But dear sweet God, she wanted this time together, she wanted the memories.

She stepped into the room, acutely aware of Jason's stare, his eyes filled with a brooding seriousness. She hesitated until he patted the spot again, then moved to sit on the edge of the bed. Jumbled thoughts, feelings, coursed through her. Yes, she wanted this, but it wasn't the same as when they'd been lovers.

Since then she'd had a child and her body had changed. Would that only anger Jason, when he saw her nude? Proof that she'd had the child he so wanted, and she'd refused him?

She hadn't had sex in nearly five years, only once after she'd had Haley and then both she and Richard had known it was only to placate Richard.

Cate shook her head, not wanting any of these thoughts intruding. She wanted only Jason. She wanted a new beginning, yet her heart knew it was only a moment, not a beginning. *No matter, any moment with Jason I'll take and keep close to my heart.*

Turning to face him, she smiled and touched his face, running her finger down his cheek, across his lips, hoping to make the seriousness disappear. Stretching out on her tummy, she felt her T-shirt inch up her back, then feather touches as he skimmed his hands across her back, over her panties, down her legs and back up.

Cate shivered under each touch, wanting his hands to stay on her body, not the delicious torture of touching, then lifting and waiting for the next touch.

Then his hands settled on her shoulders and he began to knead the knots, slowly releasing the subtle pain that had been her constant companion for the last few months. A sigh escaped her.

"Feel good?"

"You know it's marvelous."

He pressed deeper into her shoulders, working out the kinks. Then again, his hands lifted.

Only to be replaced by his mouth, kissing the sore spots, then tracing a path down her spine. She couldn't stop her reflex, and stiffened. It was only a second, but Jason felt it.

"Do you want this?" he asked, his voice husky.

Did she want this? More than breathing.

Words weren't the language of the moment. Instead she slipped off her T-shirt, flipped over and held open her arms.

Jason kneeled, straddling her body.

Cate ran her hands over his shoulders, down his arms, across his chest, storing memories. The warmth of his skin, the hard planes of his muscles and textures of his hair, crisp and sable-colored on his chest, silkier and darker as she traced the V downward … and then she hesitated before going any lower.

Keeping her gaze on his chest, she felt the warmth in her cheeks. Why should she be embarrassed now? They'd made love countless times before.

Before was the key word. So much happened between them. They were different people.

Jason nudged up her chin. "Look at me, Cat."

She raised her gaze to meet his. He didn't speak, he simply held her gaze with his, leaving the decision to take the next step up to her.

Embarrassment fled. There was no decision to make. She needed Jason as desperately as a body needed air to survive.

She moved her hands lower, teasing and provoking.

"You'll pay for that, you know." He reached across her and picked up something from the bedside table. "Close your eyes."

Her eyelids fluttered closed and she felt the cool tickle of something circle her breast. Cate looked down with a heated, heavy gaze as he circled her other breast with an orchid, then ran the exotic flower lightly down her stomach and back up, dipping lower with each pass.

The exquisite coil of tension tightened inside her. She was afraid she'd shatter before she had time to store enough memories.

Jason tucked the flower behind her ear, then retraced its route down her body with little nips, followed by tantalizing kisses, stopping long enough to completely explore her belly button.

He slid off her panties, then inched lower, and she grasped the sheets with clenched fists as the hot pressure and swirling of his tongue exploded her world.

"So not fair," she panted as the haze of passion began to clear.

He laughed, long, deep. Turning her knees to jelly again. "Have any ideas how to remedy that?"

"Nope, you?"

"Quite a few."

He held her gaze for a long, heated moment. Her breasts swelled and grew heavy, her nipples beaded under his intent scrutiny. He skimmed his fingers along the full underside of her breast, circling but not touching her nipple. First one breast, then the other.

"This is not a remedy," she complained, twisting under the renewed onslaught of erotic sensations.

Jason cupped one breast in response. "I'm not ready for a remedy just yet," he teased as he gently massaged the swollen bud of her nipple, sending a surge of heat between her thighs.

She wasn't ready for a remedy either. This night of lovemaking had to create a lifetime of memories.

In retaliation, she licked her finger and touched his nipple, savoring his shudder. She closed her eyes as he lowered his lean body on hers, and relished the sense of coming home.

"Cat," he murmured into her ear as he swiftly entered her, joining them completely.

Moving against her, inside her, heightened, lengthened her climax. She matched his heated rhythm and they journeyed together to the soaring, wondrous plane they'd visited often, long ago.

THE PHONE BEEPED AND THEN A VOICE CAME ON. "GOOD MORNING, Mr. St. Pierre, it's six o'clock. We hope you have a good day. Aloha."

Reaching across Cate, Jason fumbled with the phone, finally hitting the acknowledge key. *Reaching across Cate!*

He remembered every second of making love last night.

And afterward, he'd pulled her close, and watched her sleep in his arms and then remembered nothing more until he was awaked by the call. He'd not slept so well in years.

Cate stirred, and Jason wanted to kiss her awake, make love again, bury all memory of Richard. *But she'd said, I love you.*

Those three damning words. He'd never ask her if she'd meant him or Richard. It wasn't that he was heroic, he was chicken as hell. He didn't want to know.

And the kicker was he had no regrets about last night. None.

Period. And hoped to hell Cate had none either. *You'll find out as soon as she wakes up.*

"Hey, sleepyhead, ready to tackle a new day?"

She smiled up at him. No scurrying across the bed, no pulling up the sheet, just a sleepy wonderful smile. *There's still time, she's not awake.*

"If I have to have a wake-up call, the Halekulani sure makes it pleasant. No nasty buzzers, no pre-recorded messages." She stretched long arms and lean legs, the sheet falling away, exposing her completely.

Burning his blood.

He didn't see any embarrassment or regret on her face, nor did she make any effort to pull up the sheet. He thought about doing it himself, only for self-preservation, when the doorbell chimed.

"I guess I better get dressed," she said on a yawn.

"It's just the coffee and the popovers I ordered last night. Stay put, I'll get it."

Remembering he was nude, he shrugged off the momentary question of whether Cate would look or not, hoping she would, as he pulled the hotel robe off the bathroom door and belted it around his waist, then glanced at her.

She was full on watching him, and he wondered if she realized a tiny smile curved her lips.

He answered the door. It wasn't only their breakfast, it was the clothes he'd ordered for himself and Cate.

He wheeled in the cart and threw the zippered garment bags on the bed. "In here or on the lanai?"

"Lanai in two minutes. What's in the bags?"

"Clothes for you and me." He saw the confusion, then frustration cloud her eyes. "Cate, you didn't bring enough clothes. Hell, you know I didn't bring clothes at all."

"It'll take me forever to pay you back, but you know I'll try—"

"Cate, don't take this wrong. I don't need or want your money." He held up a hand to forestall her protest. "What I want in return is for you and Haley to be a family again. I want you to write as it's your passion and you're damned good, and I want you to be happy again. So meet me on the lanai in two or forfeit your popover."

He felt holes being drilled in his back as he wheeled the cart out the door.

12

THE POPOVERS, LIGHT AS THEY WERE, SAT LIKE A STONE ON CATE'S stomach, and the coffee burned another hole in her gut. She'd have an ulcer soon, but all the discomfort faded into the background as Jason pulled into the Kewalo Basin Harbor, and she spied Gus standing by his mustang.

It was time for more answers.

They parked beside him. "Gotta make this fast. I have a date with Grant at the Clerk of the Court's office. He's filing the Entry of Appearance as your attorney and can then get all the files. The court doesn't just issue an ex-parte order unless there are affidavits. I want to know what they used to assume Haley was in danger."

"Whatever they used is nothing but lies."

"And we're going to catch Luci and Mark out on their lies. You had a great start yesterday. Here's the bracelet, same thing as yesterday, face it toward him. And here's a recorder with Luci's little revelation on it. It's cued to the right spot, so all you have to do is hit play."

Gus pulled out another micro device and turned to Jason. "'Bro, you be with her, keep your hands out of your pockets so you don't make Mark uneasy, and use this. Nice shorts, by the way. A bit too classy, but nice."

Jason rolled his eyes as he took the recorder. "You're just jealous of my legs."

"Right," Gus grinned. "Now, your recorder is voice-activated from Cate's bracelet, so don't fidget with it, though if he's smart, he'll know we're gonna record him—after all, we got Luci. But I'm betting you'll rattle him pretty good, so he'll forget."

Cate clasped the bracelet back on and gingerly handled the recorder.

"Okay, both of you?"

They nodded.

"Good. See the blue building? That's the contest HQ. They board the dive boat in about twenty minutes. Your man is in the building already, checking his gear. He doesn't look upset, so Luci didn't squeal. Here are passes to get you inside. Got my cell, call me if you run into issues. Otherwise I'll check in with you a bit before noon."

With a wave, he slid behind the Mustang's wheel and drove off.

"Phew. Did you get all that?" Cate asked Jason.

"Pretty much. Are you up for this?"

She raised her fists in the air, Rocky style. "You betcha. Let's go ruin his day."

Marching to the building, she flashed her pass, marveling that Gus thought of everything. Even in the sea of wet suits, media and guests, it wasn't hard to find Mark. He was taller than most and brilliantly blond.

Most of the diver's wetsuits had their nation's flags printed on the chest or back, and some suits were embellished with corporate advertising. Mark's suit was plain, except for the word "Luci" running down one sleeve, and the universal sign for a diver—white diagonal stripe on a red border—running down the other sleeve.

His back was turned. Jason moved to one side of him, Cate the other. She tapped Mark on the shoulder. He looked, whirled around and nearly dropped his mask.

Cate touched the "Luci" on his arm. "Interesting. We need to talk, now."

Mark's glance skittered between her and Jason. "You're here. We didn't think—"

"Ah, and I thought you were bright," Cate put a finger to her brow. "Like I said, we need to have a little chat, now."

Mark looked at his gear, then back at her.

"You do understand I don't care if you miss your dive. We can talk here or outside. I'd suggest outside."

He picked up his tanks and dive bag.

"Leave it," Jason suggested.

"No, sir. This *is* a competition. I'd never leave my gear."

"Don't 'sir' me. It denotes respect, and you sure as hell don't have any for me or Cate."

"And it's interesting to see what you value and will protect," Cate added.

She led the way out of the building, and Jason followed Mark. They found a spot near a moored and currently vacant glass-bottom tour boat. It was as quiet as they were going to get.

"Listen to this carefully before you say another word." Cate brought out the recorder and held it up so Mark couldn't miss a word, then pressed play.

Mark blanched, hearing Luci's soulless destruction of his love followed by her fervent declaration of love for Richard, but it was Luci's spitting out the letters spelling divorce that had him sagging against the boat's ramp. "How'd you get that."

"How doesn't matter. You know it's Luci and the tape hasn't been tampered with. You were duped, deceived, hoodwinked, taken advantage of, and used. You went along with this insane scheme for what? The love of a good woman? Money?"

"It is all legal."

"How is lying to my daughter to make her believe she was only going on a vacation, kidnapping her, transporting her across state lines legal? I don't know how you lied your way out of criminal charges. And worse, you knew all along what was planned and yet you made me think she might come back? Even making PBJs for her?"

"What did the Malloys offer you, Mark?" Jason asked.

"Enough money to open my own dive shop, here." He buried his face in splayed fingers, Cate saw the shimmer of tears. They didn't move her at all. "How could I have missed Luci and Richard together? How could we make love while she loved another man? How could she make all these plans with me, knowing it was all ..."

"A lie? Simple. You were a tool. Luci said it best."

"I loved her."

Cate rolled her eyes, making Jason laugh.

Mark fisted his hands.

"Don't be more stupid. I wasn't laughing at you, but love. What it makes people do."

Cate's heart squeezed. She'd turned Jason into a cynic about love.

"Adams? We're loading now," one of the contest directors called.

Mark waved him off.

Cate recalled Gus's words about videotaping. "Did you videotape me at any time?"

Deeper anguish twisted Mark's face.

"Luci doesn't love you. Make this work for you ... and me and Haley, now. It's not a question of anything being legal, it's a question of morals and responsibility."

Mark said nothing and she was afraid she'd pushed too hard.

"Yes, I filmed you. At your new apartment building, the old guy that Haley was afraid of? And at the pool and in the kitchen, that little fire? And when you were in LA, I filmed Haley alone. Maybe a dozen different times, maybe more. Whenever Luci asked me, I ran over, using some excuse. You even saw me at the house, but never questioned it—"

Mark broke off as the contest director walked over. "Are you diving?" the man asked.

"No."

"You're the leader. It's all on the line today."

Mark looked as his feet as he shook his head slowly.

"You understand you'll lose all points—"

"Yes, and I'm not diving."

The contest director walked away, turned back once, then got on the dive boat.

"We need you to make a statement. You can come with us now and put it on tape and paper, or believe me, we'll find you and make you do this in court," Jason threatened.

Cate didn't know if any of that was true, but it sounded really good.

THE SUITE'S DOOR CHIMED. JASON LEFT CATE AND MARK ON THE lanai and opened the door to Gus. Jason put a finger to his lips, and mouthed "Mark."

Gus raised his eyebrows and signaled for Jason to take the lead.

As Jason made the introductions, he watched Gus turn from nice guy with a ready smile into a stern, hard, investigator.

"Adams," Gus said simply, each syllable dripping with disdain.

"He's handwritten his statement, and I wanted you to read it before he signed it. We have it on tape as well," Jason said.

Gus read it quickly and completely, nodding as he read. "I glanced through the court documents and this makes sense. Sad, sick sense."

Mark was looking out toward the ocean, but Jason knew he was listening. "What do we do with him?"

"Sir—Mr. St. Pierre. I have nothing left in Colorado, and this is where I want to be. You can find me if you need to at the White Stripe Dive Shop off of Puuhale Road. It's mine."

Jason looked at Gus, not wanting to trust Mark one bit.

Gus looked at Cate, then Mark. "Sign, then go. But leave Hawai'i and we'll find you."

Mark signed the statement and got up to leave. He opened his mouth to say something, then shut it quickly, as if sensing the magnitude of the hostility shimmering in the air.

Gus showed him out, then came back and opened his satchel. "The Malloys are cocky, absolutely sure you'd come at some point, Cate, and they covered all their bases. But they didn't expect Jason to help you get here as fast as you did, and they didn't expect me," he said with a grin. "Before I show you what I found, think we could get some beers and coffee and maybe some sandwiches? Breakfast was a long time ago."

Jason intercepted Gus's look. There was another bombshell coming, and he wanted time for Mark to be gone and Cate to simmer down before he delivered the next round of bad news.

Jason made the call, and they waited for the food. And waited again while Gus took his first bite.

"Okay, I know you're stalling. Just give it to me straight," Cate said.

"I told you, you can work for me any time." Gus pulled out a stack of paper and a DVD. "Did you recently tell Haley she was going to her grandparents for a vacation?"

"Of course not. First, I couldn't afford it, and second, you saw how they acted around Haley—they're not the doting type of grandparents."

"Apparently Luci convinced Haley that's what was happening and you were coming later. The Malloys were cutting it close. Luci's detour to Steamboat put the schedule back. They had an appointment with a child psychologist planned for Monday, cancelled, rebooked for Tuesday around noon—"

"That's what Haley meant when she said she'd seen a doctor. She didn't look sick and wasn't hot, so I thought she was confused about the doctor."

Jason watched Cate carefully, knowing how painful it was for her to be the victim of such constructed deceit, layered with enough truth to make it pass the smell test.

He reached for her hand and held it. Cate's smile was worth the impetuous gesture.

"The psychologist's affidavit states that Haley appeared to be afraid of moving from Highgate, her home." Gus started reading the report out loud: "That Haley Marie Malloy stated she would be leaving the only friends she had. The new apartment was scary, and going to day care meant she'd never have time with her mommy. Starting kindergarten scared her too. Her daddy was dead, and now mommy was too busy to be her mommy anymore."

Gus looked at Cate. "The psychologist also noted that Haley appears to be very underweight by best practice medical height and weight standards. His recommendation was to remove Haley from your custody." He finished reciting the report: "Based upon my evaluation, it is my professional opinion that placement of the child with her grandparents, Helene and Harve Malloy, would be in the child's best interests."

Jason felt Cate's grip tighten on his hand. She swallowed repeatedly. "Do you want to stop for a while?" he asked.

"No, get it all out, then we'll see what can be done. I hate the bastards, and if I think I'm going to throw up, I'll run for the bathroom, so don't be surprised."

Jason leaned and kissed her forehead, not caring that Gus was in the room.

"Do you think the psychologist was paid by the Malloys?"

"Honestly? No. Could they have led him to the conclusion they wanted? It's not ethical, but it is done, especially if there is just enough to go on. And before I play these, I want to warn you, these vids are not so pretty," Gus said, pulling out a small portable DVD player.

"You mean worse than what you've just told us?" Cate asked.

"Yeah, this is the physical evidence the Malloys used to convince the judge to grant the temporary order."

The video was fairly clear though for some reason Cate had expected it to be grainy. It showed Haley backing up and hiding around her as an old man shuffled along the balcony from his apartment to the stairway. He had longish gray hair, his clothes were wrinkled but not dirty.

"That's old man Wilson," Cate exclaimed. "The first time Haley saw him, she was shy, as she usually is, but she wasn't afraid of him. His wife of sixty years recently passed away and he's lonely. Remember, Jason, my landlady even said Mr. Wilson was wondering where Haley was?"

There were assorted videos of Haley waking up at night, crying, calling for her mother, and no mother came. "It's not true, in fact, she'd sleep the rest of the night with me. Sometime with one of Richard's shirts tucked in next to her."

There were videos of Haley alone in the pool, the deck surrounding the pool panned by the camera, and showing it empty. No adult supervision. "I never leave Haley alone in the water. Never. She knew it too. She wouldn't go in without one of us there. The only time Richard ever gave her a swat on her little behind was when she didn't wait for us and got into the water."

There were others, Haley alone in the Range Rover, windows rolled up. Cate asleep in a park while Haley played nearby. All the ways possible to make her look neglectful and putting her child at risk.

"Mark did a good job on the videos, I'd be concerned. What a bastard," Cate said.

Gus stopped the playback. He paused.

"What?"

"There is one more. This one is hard to watch, it's the fire in the kitchen."

Cate took a deep breath as Gus started up the video again.

Luci and Haley were making dinner. "When is Mommy coming," Haley asked, standing on a little footstool, stirring a pot of something. The camera panned to Luci and she shrugged, "When she gets back, from wherever she is *this* time."

Haley frowned, her bottom lip poking out and Luci went over to give her a hug. Then the burner flames up and Haley screamed. Luci pulled her away and put out the fire.

"Stop. Gus, can you play that back, slower?"

He did.

"There! Did you see it? Luci put the bread on or near the burner so it would catch fire. She could have really hurt Haley if the flames had caught her clothes or hair." Cate jumped up and stormed around in tight circles. "I ran in as soon as I heard Haley scream. I was packing for the move, Luci promised to teach Haley how to make a pasta sauce. God, the Malloys must hate me to go to such lengths."

"You're dealing with egocentric maniacs here. They thought these kinds of tricks would only be looked at on the surface, mostly, I'm assuming, because of who they are and because you couldn't immediately be here to fight this. Which they'd use as another point in their case that you're not fit to care for Haley," Jason said.

"Being poor isn't a reason." But Cate knew Jason was right on part of it, the Malloys were egocentric, even dynastic, but she'd done harm to Richard by not loving him. And in turn, she'd done harm to Haley, which was the total opposite of what she'd been attempting by staying in a loveless marriage for her daughter's sake.

Time to get back to the crisis at hand. "Mark said he'd do whatever, whenever Luci wanted him to do something," Cate said.

"He was gone a lot last month. Said it was diving related. And since he kept everything like a well-oiled machine at the house, I didn't mind."

"Luci must have called him every time she thought there was a good photo op, and he'd be there. I'm surprised I didn't see him. And he was over at Highgate all the time. I didn't think anything about it." She shook her head.

"Since we have Mark's statement that he fixed the vids and pix, we'll go over all of it this weekend and look for tampering," Gus said. "It's not always easy to find, but I have great guys who are experts at video forensics. Then we can offer the tampering as evidence to the court on the motion to vacate the order."

Gus picked up the sheaf of legal documents, quickly thumbed through them, then abruptly stopped. Cate again felt the nausea burn her throat.

"What?"

"The date of the permanent order is set." He began reading it aloud. "The Permanent Custody Order hearing for Haley Marie Malloy will be heard in Family Court, Kapolei Court Complex, 3rd Floor, 4673 Kapolei Parkway, Kapolei, HI 96707-3272, on August 27, 10 a.m."

The silence in the room was deafening. They could hear the splashing in the pool below.

"That's this Monday," Jason said.

Cate couldn't stand still and paced the lanai. "Can we win with what we have?"

"We have the custom of *ho'oponopono* in Hawai'i ," Gus countered. "Righting a wrong through group effort. That's what we have now, a group effort."

"Luci will be on the Malloys' side, we have Mark," Cate said.

"You keep forgetting, me, Gus and Grant, and most of all, you," Jason added.

Gus buckled his empty satchel, "I'm leaving you this set of files and videos, along with the player. Both Grant and I have copies."

Cate looked at them with revulsion. "Thanks, Gus."

He raised a brow.

"No, seriously, thank you. I'll start believing in *ho'oponopono*."

Gus left and Cate returned to the table to read the papers herself, slowly, trying to marshal her thoughts into a direction, instead of churning with chaos and fear.

"I wonder how that child psychologist got Haley to say I was too busy to be her mommy anymore. I wonder if Luci fed her those thoughts."

"It's possible it was her way of trying to cut the bond. You said Haley and Richard were close, and I know you and Haley are, but you rarely use the word family when talking about the three of you."

Putting down the papers, she tipped Jason's chin upward. "Do you want to hear this?"

His eyes turned from whiskey to muddy brown, showing her clearly the war going on between brain and heart.

"I honestly don't know. Do I?"

"It'll never be the right time, but you have the right to know."

"Right?"

"Yes. God knows how it was that you came along in your car when you did, but you've been in this since the start. You've pushed and pulled me along, you've seen the worst and you've stayed, when I would have expected you to walk away. After all, it's not like we've been friends for the past years."

He leaned back in his chair and crossed his arms, while his gaze remained pinned to hers, nodding for her to continue.

"This whole thing didn't come around simply because Richard and I disagreed on most everything—there's more to it. I just didn't realize it until Luci yelled it on the beach."

"You're talking about the divorce?"

She nodded and swallowed hard, uncertain that revealing the truth was the wise course. "As you said, Haley adored her father. She was too young to be at the funeral and stayed that day at the Malloys' estate. Of course she knew something was wrong and kept asking for her daddy. I told her Daddy had an accident and was with the angels in Heaven. One day a month or so ago, she told me she was sure she'd seen her daddy in the forest behind the house. I asked her how, and she said a baby deer looked at her the same way Daddy did."

Cate breathed deep and looked at her clenched fists, consciously making an effort to flex her fingers.

"What I'm telling you is the absolute truth." She waited a beat and stared directly at Jason, daring him to check for the telltale twitch. "I never loved Richard, but I love Haley with every fiber of my being. She was born because of a mistake."

Jason's silence was expected. She took another deep breath and plowed onward, knowing she might well be killing the easier camaraderie budding between them.

"You probably won't remember this, but there was an opening at the Denver Art Museum a few months after we'd ...

after I left you, and I was Richard's date. You had some tall, sexy blonde on your arm. You and I smiled politely at each other, and I couldn't wait to leave. Richard took me back to Highgate. We finished the night with several bottles of wine and sex. And when we ran out of protection, Haley. It's not pretty, but it's the truth."

Jason looked away, and she gave him time to assimilate the truth. "I can stop now, you have the basic facts."

"Continue," he said as he again met her gaze.

"I never asked Richard why he wanted to date me. He'd started asking me out as soon as he found out we'd... I was available, but if I had to guess it would be the whole competition thing with you he was always battling. Another positive trait the Malloys instilled in him."

Jason nodded slowly, as if what she was saying made sense to him. "Shortly after you dumped me, he started ratcheting up that whole competition crap. I fought him to get anything done and it only got worse. That's why I eventually dissolved the partnership," he said.

"It wasn't just that." Cate couldn't sit there another minute and moved back to the lanai railing, wishing she had an open space where she could pace as she confessed. Instead, she leaned back against the railing, facing him. "When I realized I was pregnant, I was going to get rid of it. No adoption, no social services for this child. But Richard kept after me, telling me constantly that we could make it work. He wanted a child to carry on the name, the dynasty and for whatever reason, he wanted me, at least at that point."

"God, Cate, you're a strong woman, you could have done ... that without him knowing."

"Except I had horrible morning sickness that lasted all day. I wasn't eating, the meds didn't help, it wasn't pretty in my apartment—basically it was awful. Richard was there, taking care of me, even taking me to the hospital when I got too dehydrated. And then it was too late. I was past that point.

"Richard wanted to marry me, and I sure as hell wasn't going to raise a child by myself ... and somehow I knew he'd be a good father, so it seemed the best solution. I knew I didn't love him"— *I've only ever loved you*—"and as I said, I'm not sure he loved me. I never heard him say he did. The Malloys hated that we married in a small civil service."

"No big church wedding for the heir to the fortune?" Jason asked.

She shook her head and ignored his mocking tone. "And while I had the Pulitzer, I brought nothing to the marriage, nothing that mattered to them, anyway."

"And why did you leave me?"

"Jason, I'm not sure—"

"I'm a big boy, I can handle it."

She'd been dreading this question for years.

He didn't move, his gaze laser sharp.

"Jace, you're successful at what you do because you have an immense drive. You are the most dynamic person I've ever known. You take charge, you know what's right—"

"But?"

She tried to get the words through the thickness in her throat. Swallowing didn't help. Then the dam opened. "But you didn't hear me." The words poured out. "We'd talk and talk, and you'd listen as we shared plans. But you didn't *hear* that my choice was to wait to have a child, no matter how many times I told you. Then I realized all your successes came from that same drive and tenacity to make things work the way you thought they should. I knew I couldn't fight something so deeply a part of you. And I realized I couldn't take the chance that you wouldn't understand. I was so afraid of having a baby, someone who was completely dependent on me.

"I couldn't change you and I couldn't change me."

She paused, drained and afraid. "And now, when it's too late, we're both different people, and we could have made it work." Not able to witness his ramrod straight back, the up-tilt of his chin, his crossed arms for another second, she closed her eyes.

Then she heard the slam of a door.

The humid air pressed down her as she opened her eyes to an empty chair.

What the heck did you expect? Stupid girl.

STUPID MAN, WHAT THE HELL WERE YOU THINKING? DID YOU REALLY want to hear a single word about Richard and Cate's life together? How Haley was conceived? Why Cate left?

No! He wasn't masochistic, yet he'd stayed until he'd heard "too late... we could have made it work."

It sure as hell was too late. Damn her.

He needed space and speed, and drove the rental Mustang too fast up the Pali. The rush of the wind felt good, and when the Friday commuting traffic began to get heavier, he weaved between the cars, not really caring that he was being the epitome of a tourist.

By the time he got to the other side and Kailua, he headed straight for the beach. It was a long stretch of sand and usually never as busy as Waikiki.

He sat on a cement picnic table watching the gentle swell of the waves. Cate had said he had a right to know and had given him the choice to listen.

Her confession, spoken low, had been filled with such anguish that he didn't doubt for a second it was all true.

And for the umpteenth time, he thought back to what he'd imagined had been his perfect life with Cate. This time he ruthlessly applied the same precision he used to analyze complex deals, removing layer upon layer of emotion, and looked at the facts.

He'd been filled with heady success. He'd outgrown his investment banking career, decided to strike out with a partnership and found Richard.

Richard had the money and knowledge, even the instinct for the deal, and at first, the all-crucial drive. They'd generated venture capital to tech start-ups, then bought bolder stakes in companies, then bigger acquisitions.

Buy, sell, incubate and manipulate.

Everything he'd worked for was within reach. And while Cate had been waffling about having a family, he'd been so sure he'd convinced her of his need ..."

His need!

Was it true? Everything he'd done, all the skills he'd honed, his very persona had pushed away the woman he'd loved?

Shaky nausea roiled through him. He wanted to ignore her words, forget what he'd heard, but knew it was impossible.

Six years ago, after the shock had worn off that Cate had actually left him, his anger consumed him, and it only got worse when he'd seen her on Richard's arm, learning of their marriage, her pregnancy, all in such short order.

He'd lost faith that the love he'd felt had ever been reciprocated.

But eventually, with Marta's help, he'd begun to make changes in his life. He'd found a sort of happy balance between the fast, tense, deadlines of a deal and the slowness of cooking, the sweat of running a 10K, and the dreams of Cate that still haunted him at night.

Memories were a blessing and a curse. Self-preservation was finding a balance between the two.

It was time again to reweave the cloak of self-preservation, until he had time to sort through all she'd said. Anger did little, and since his other coping mechanisms weren't available to him, he needed to run.

Taking off his flip-flops and leaving them on the sand, not caring that his khaki shorts weren't optimum gear, he started to run, using the wet sand from the gentle tide to give him firm purchase and let him move as fast as his legs would pump. He threw off his belt, opened his shirt and ran faster, feeling the endorphins flush the stress away, filling him with nearly invincible courage.

Running still faster, he reached the end of the beach, turned around and ran flat out until he spied his belt on the sand. Winded, sweaty and pumped, he jogged to his flip-flops, and then headed for the shave ice truck, once again a master at self-preservation.

He would finish this and then move on with his life once again without Cate. And as he'd done once before, he'd deal with the lonely nights.

13

WAITING FOR JASON IN THE LOBBY PROBABLY WASN'T THE SMARTEST thing to do, but Cate hoped she'd see him return. And she needed company, at least the buzz of people around her. The suite, as nice as it was, had become smaller and smaller as the hours passed.

Friday night was busy with chattering guests, party goers, and a formal Japanese-clad wedding party, yet she still felt alone in the crowd. She yearned for Haley, knowing if she were here, she'd be making up stories about this or that person, and she'd have loved seeing the wedding kimono.

They'd often made up stories about anything that caught their fancy. Just two weeks ago Haley had seen a pocket dog in a purse. She'd thought it so silly and cute, and called the dog Muffin. She said Muffin must be that small because it was a magical creature. The woman carrying it had to guard it from the evil gnomes who wanted the creature for their own use. Haley had even pointed out that it wore a diamond collar and had a single black mark on its forehead, proof to her it was from the land of fairy magic. Just like all the books Cate had read to her.

Cate rapidly blinked back tears, trying hard to recapture the belief she'd have her back in her arms Monday.

Finally, after her umpteenth cup of coffee, and the beginnings of a numb rear end, she saw Jason stride through the doors.

Rumpled and sandy, he looked delicious, and so thought most of the other women in the lobby who gave him more than a second glance.

Cate remained seated in her chair, not wanting to draw his attention, relieved that he was okay after all she'd dumped on him hours earlier. Even so, he stopped mid stride, turned and stared directly at her. No smile, but no resentment either.

She might want more, but she'd take neutral.

"It's nearly midnight," he said by way of greeting.

"I ... just needed to make sure you were safe."

"Being a mom?"

No, lover. Cate shrugged, letting him think it was true.

"I went up and over the Pali, took a long run in Kailua, ate shave ice, went back up the Pali and sat at the overlook for hours. We'll win Monday, Cate. The Malloys are sleazy and thought they'd nailed it. Mark is their weak link, because nobody counted on Luci's emotions blowing it."

He sat on the chair next to her. "The next two days are going to be long, so I thought we could use a diversion. Do you think Sunday is enough time for us to go over the papers one more time? Because I chartered a helicopter for the day tomorrow so we can island hop. You mentioned something about never really seeing the islands."

She stared at him, mouth open. This wasn't what she'd expected. She'd worried that he might despise her, or had been so angry he'd have an accident. Or even for his own sanity, that he'd leave her in Gus's capable hands to see this nightmare through, while he'd flee Hawai'i . She wouldn't have blamed him.

But certainly not something so thoughtful, so kind.

"If you'd rather not and want to stay close, I can cancel, but they did say turbulence shouldn't be an issue," he added with the slightest of smiles.

"I'd love to island hop. I didn't want to stare at four walls and simply worry. I can't see Haley and it's killing me, but I can't change that until we win on Monday."

"I'm glad you're thinking victory."

"We have to, there's no other choice, right? So, the island tour is perfect. Thank you."

His smile reached his eyes, but didn't linger. The 'copter's going to be ready at ten tomorrow and the charter company has breakfast, lunch and dinner planned, all on different islands. So, let's hit the sack, er, let's get some sleep."

Cate swallowed the lump, knowing last night was the last time they'd be together, wholly joined. She held out her hand. Jason hauled her off the chair and they headed to the suite.

Hand on the doorknob of her bedroom, she glanced back to see Jason staring at her. He touched his forehead with two fingers, giving her a quick salute, and ducked into his room.

She closed the door behind her and slipped under the sheets, alone.

A CLASSIC ISLAND BREAKFAST OF RICE, EGGS AND PORTUGUESE sausage, hot coffee and guava juice, waited for them on a picnic table under palm trees.

And an orchid lei. Jason placed it around Cate's neck. "Aloha."

It was a perfect day, and he had every intention of making

sure he and Cate enjoyed it. Sunday was a work day, and Monday was the day Cate was going to be reunited with Haley and it would all be over. He'd be gone. Life would circle around.

Cate had on the white shorts and simple yellow T-shirt he'd bought, and they fitted perfectly, both in size and style.

They met TC, their pilot, and boarded the Eco-Star helicopter then floated off the ground. Within minutes they were listening to the history of Hawai'i as they flew over Pearl Harbor and the Arizona Memorial, past Diamond Head, Hanauma Bay, and to the windward side, along the verdant green of the steep Ko'olua cliffs and past Chinaman's Hat.

"Haley would love to see that," Cate said into the microphone, pointing to the small island shaped like its name. "She'd have great fun making up stories."

"Do you think she'll become a writer?" Jason asked, realizing he really wanted to know.

"I don't know. It'll be interesting and fun to see how she grows up."

Jason kept looking at the funny little island below, remembering he'd agreed with himself that he'd be gone after Monday and wouldn't be around to see Haley grow up.

The helicopter sped over the ocean toward Maui, skirting Molokai and Lanai. Landing on the slopes of the crater Haleakala, at the Ulupalakua Ranch.

Cate and Jason stretched their legs and lunched on beef tenderloin sandwiches at the picnic table sitting in the shade of the ranch store's veranda.

"It's kinda cool to see the red dirt of the crater and cactus on a ranch after all the green."

"When you said you'd never seen the other islands, I didn't realize you'd never been to the ranch either," Jason said, surprised.

"No, Haley and I never came with Richard. The first time was for his funeral. Back home, Haley would chatter on about seeing the hula. I guess the Malloys' housekeeper took her to a hula show that day to keep her occupied... oh my God. That's why it was so easy to convince her to come. She's been wanting to come back ever since and dance the hula again.

"I'm sorry, I know you wanted this to be a distraction and it's the most amazing trip, but my little one—"

"I know, she's in your mind all the time. Mine too," Jason said, touching Cate's hand briefly.

"I wonder if Richard would have tried to get full custody."

Jason looked at her sadly, sure that would have been Richard's intent, or at least he'd want Haley to live with him in Hawai'i , which would be harder for Cate to visit or have Haley for visitation.

"Yeah, I think so too."

She knew what he'd been thinking, and it shouldn't surprise him. It had always been like that until she'd blown his world away. He hadn't seen that coming.

They had a little time before the tour continued, so ate ice cream cones and wandered the red-dirt paths to see the view of the ocean from two thousand feet up.

Aboard the Eco-Star again, they flew over West Maui's valleys and rainforests, watching as idyllic waterfalls cascaded over the cliff edges, down into the streams running along the rainforest floor. They flew over coastline of Hana and the hundreds of waterfalls in its rainforest, then over and around the Haleakala crater itself.

Cate pointed to the small figures below. "You can hike down there?"

"Yup, and camp," their pilot answered. "There are three wilderness cabins. It can get down to thirty degrees at night, kinda like your mountains in summer. The elevation of the crater is a tad over ten thousand feet."

And onward over the Alenuihaha Channel to the Big Island and down the West side of the Island, over Ai'opio Beach with the remnants of ancient fish traps in the bay. Through the high valley between Mauna Kea and Mauna Loa volcanos.

"Am I seeing two kinds of textures to the lava?" Cate asked.

"Good eyes. The smooth undulating areas are *pahoehoe,* and the jagged, rocky lava is called *a'a,*" TC replied.

"I love it. You'd say 'ah ah' every time you'd step on a piece," Jason quipped, earning a smile and a head shake from Cate. So worth the terrible pun.

Dinner at Volcano House perched on the edge of the caldera was perfect. Bowls of simple saimin noodles topped with pork followed by papaya boats and toffee macadamia cookies. "I'm in heaven," Cate said, elbows on the table, cradling a cup of coffee.

"We've saved the most dramatic for last." Jason checked his itinerary. "Costal East rift zone, the Kilauea caldera, lava flows and plumes. It's going to just be dusk when we head over them, so we should really be able to see the plumes and the flows."

"Lava scares the bejesus out of me. I can't wait to see this! Let's hope Madam Pele has a spectacle for us," Cate said with a shiver. She picked up the last bite of cookie and held it up to his lips.

A gesture made countless times before. He remembered the vow he'd made only last night on the beach, to draw the cloak of self-preservation around him, remembering it was also a game of balance.

And of time. There was little left with her.

He opened his lips and gently took the bite. "You're going to regret giving me that," he warned.

"I may never eat again. This has been quite the sightseeing adventure. Thank you again for helping me get through the waiting."

Her wistful smile twisted his heart a little bit more.

TC joined them. "Ready for the finale?"

"Bring it on, Pele," Cate said.

The 'copter flew as close as safely possible to the plumes and flows of lava, glowing orange in the waning light. It was primitive and primal.

All too soon, they turned northwest and toward Oahu.

As they crested Diamond Head, the city of Honolulu lay below them like a glittering jewel perched at the edge of black velvet, the ocean. Very spectacular.

The ride back to the hotel was quiet. "Tired?" Jason asked Cate.

"A bit."

Back in the suite, Cate hovered outside her bedroom door.

"Did you need something?" he asked.

"Yes. No. I mean, thank you again for today. You know Haley is never far from my mind ... but today was wonderful." She took a step toward him.

It took every ounce of control for him not to pick her up and carry her into his bedroom. But he couldn't. He could take a bite of cookie, he could sip from her glass, hold her hand, but he couldn't make love with her again and not have her forever.

"Sleep well," he said, moving toward his own bedroom. Then he turned back, and in two steps reached her, held her close for a moment, kissed her hair, and gently pushed her away. "It was a good day."

ANOTHER MORNING IN PARADISE.

Truly, it was a beautiful morning and the old saying fit. Jason woke up early, leaving a note for Cate to meet him by the pool.

He didn't need to see the videos again, but he did want to

comb through the hearing file at least one more time before he and Cate went over it together.

Feeling pretty confident their side was solid, he nevertheless wouldn't be surprised if the Malloys pulled a rabbit out of their vast hat of tricks. Maybe he should call Gus and set up a meet with Grant. It felt a bit too abrupt to meet the first time at the courthouse.

A shadow fell over his lounger. Rolling his head to the side, he saw tanned long legs. His gaze moved up to the hem of the bright blue and green drapey thing the store clerk called a pareo, now wrapped around Cate, knotted at her neck. She looked like a beach goddess. "Sleep well?

"Actually yes. I'm sorry I'm late, I had to exchange the bikini."

"Too skimpy?"

"No, too small. I love the style."

"Well then, let's see it." He knew damn well he was only torturing himself but was sure it'd be worth it.

Cate pulled up her sunglasses, looking at him askance. "Seriously?"

"It's a pool, and it's not busy yet. Yeah."

She untied the fabric around her neck and threw it at him.

Laughing, he pulled what seemed like yards of fabric off his face to find her sleek body covered, barely, and only in the places that had to be covered for the public. Thin strips covered her breasts and two triangles barely covered her butt and front. The suit had big gold rings holding the scraps of fabric together, and on Cate, it was unbelievably sexy. And right. "Turn around."

"Oh, come on."

He whirled his finger in a circle and she pirouetted, then grabbed the pareo off his lounger and wrapped herself in it. "Coffee?"

"You are so predictable. On the table behind you."

He watched Cate pour a cup, brown arms strong and slim. She sat on the lounger next to him, pointing to the stack of papers.

"Just going over them again. I need to meet with Grant—"

"You want to see his game plan."

"I've read the pages and seen the strategy the Malloys used, and I want to make sure we counter it strongly enough."

"Jace, neither of us can know. We've got a good group, you pulled Gus in, brilliant move, and he pulled in his team. We have the truth on our side. Am I scared? You bet."

"Which is why I want to talk to Grant."

Two more shadows blocked his sun. "Tourists!" Gus said in mock displeasure. "I called the room, no answer, and no answer on your cell, so we decided to drop by."

Jason checked his pockets and the satchel, no phone. "Damn, left it in the car. It was late last night when we got in."

"Hawai'i makes you forget a lot. That's our plan. Relax, spend money, forget work."

"Isn't there a Hawaiian word for that one?" Cate asked.

"Yeah, but it's too long. Let me introduce Grant Bollister."

Jason stood and shook the lawyer's hand.

"I was going to call you later today," Jason said.

"Bro, I know you," Gus said. "And Grant wanted to meet you both before the hearing, so here we are. No stuffy offices for us Hawaiians."

Gus handed Cate a small stack of photographs. "Haley's okay, Cate. Confused and asking for you all the time, but she's outside playing with the nanny, or whoever Emme is. They went shelling yesterday and today are snorkeling."

Jason watched Cate carefully as she devoured each picture, touching it softly before handing it to him. She didn't cry, but he could see that she ached.

"Thank you. I didn't expect this. It's bittersweet but wonderful. How do you know she's asking for me?"

"Parabolic microphone. My guy in the boat has one. We only use it when someone is outside."

"Is there a place with a bigger table so we can spread out?" Grant asked.

Jason called over a waiter, who found them a large, secluded table and brought more coffee and cups.

For two hours Cate answered Grant's questions about each incident which had photographic evidence, telling him the truth about what each picture really was supposed to show, about why she thought the child psychologist said what he did, and about what she knew of their finances. And then about her pregnancy and Richard's constant care.

Cate had been determined to start out the day on a positive note, but now she was drained and worried. "Can we win this, Grant?"

"Gus's guys have found most of the tampering spots in the videos and photographs. Mark was good or had good equipment. Gus's team is better. We have the recordings and Mark's statement." He looked at each of them. "I suggest you all arrive about 9:45. Dress conservatively, no slacks. It will be Cate and me at the table. Jason, you and Gus will sit behind us in the witness area. I'm going back to the office and call the Malloys' attorney, suggest we talk—"

"Talk? As in compromise? I don't want a compromise, I want Haley back. There never should have been a custody hearing—she's mine." Cate's stomach clenched. She wouldn't have Jason beside her during the hearing, Grant wouldn't say they'd win, and it all seemed way too real. Yesterday's tour felt light-years ago.

"Not a compromise, Cate—"

"Excuse me." She quickly pushed back her chair and fled to

the ladies room. Stomach heaving, she entered the stall in the nick of time.

Fifteen minutes later, she came out to find Jason waiting outside the door. "They're gone."

"I'm sorry, it all just hit me so hard, so real, and then Grant wouldn't say we'd win."

Jason gave her a lopsided smile. "Cate, attorneys never tell their clients they're going to win. They don't like to be sued. If you feel like it, we've got to pick out our court clothes."

After another draining hour making sure she looked conservative enough in the cream skirt topped with a black and cream top and black peep-toed shoes, Cate wanted nothing more than this day to be over.

They carried their packages upstairs. "I'm going to take a nap," Cate said, still slightly queasy.

Deep inside she wanted to believe that Haley would be in her arms very soon. But the specter of having to deal with the Malloys on their home territory, even in front of an impartial judge, was terrifying.

She fell asleep with *ho‘oponopono* on her lips.

14
_____

ENTERING THE WIDE DOORS OF THE FAMILY COURTHOUSE, CATE itched to wipe her damp palms on her skirt, but the sweat would show badly on the cream fabric, and she didn't want the Malloys to see an ounce of fear.

Jason pulled a pristine handkerchief out his pocket and handed it to her.

"I didn't know men still carried these," she said.

"They come in handy. No purses for us manly men to carry those little Kleenex packets," he joked.

She was grateful beyond measure he was here with her, sensing every nuance of her tension and doing his best to lessen it.

And he'd reminded her just before they entered the courthouse to believe. Just believe. Then brushed her forehead with a butterfly kiss.

Up on the third floor, after checking in at the bailiff's station, Cate and Jason waited near courtroom 3A. They were early, but neither she nor Jason wanted to hang around the hotel waiting.

Shortly, Gus joined them, dressed in an understated sports

coat and khakis, and Grant appeared moments later dressed in a conservative blue suit, toting his big lawyer's briefcase.

Benches lined the hall and windows, but Cate couldn't sit. This was it. This was the moment that never should have happened, to fight for her daughter, taken by people, family no less, who had their own agenda for Haley.

Instead of watching the growing crowd in an attempt to settle her nerves, Cate watched Jason. He looked strong, sophisticated and rock steady. The white of his shirt contrasted deeply with the tan on his face and hands. The regimental tie, navy sports jacket and gray slacks fitted him perfectly. He wore board shorts or business attire with the same aplomb.

She closed her eyes and attempted to recapture the warmth of Jason's lips on her forehead.

Feeling a hand squeeze her shoulder, she opened her eyes to see the Malloys stride down the hall, flanked by three lawyers. Looking nearly regal, they swept by her team with barely a look.

They stopped at the courtroom door, as apparently the leader of their cadre of suits went to check them in at the bailiff's station.

Grant joined the attorney at the station and was soon deep in conversation. He broke off when the bailiff interrupted him and pointed to the door. Grant nodded to the other attorney, then joined Cate, Jason and Gus. "Court's about to be in session. We're first—let's go."

"What were you talking about?"

The Malloys led the procession into the courtroom and Grant couldn't answer her.

True to the movies, there was the classic swinging gate that separated the gallery from the court. Cate followed Grant as he moved to the right table. The Malloys had the left table along with their lead attorney; the other two sat behind.

Gus and Jason sat behind her and Grant, and though she'd tried to not turn and look at them, she caved.

Gus smiled and Jason nodded. She could hear his voice again, saying "Believe."

The court clerk entered and placed a pile of files on the judge's desk.

"It's about to start," Grant whispered to her. "Just follow my lead. It'll surprise you, but play it cool."

She took a deep breath, worrying just how he was going to surprise her. *Remember ho'oponopono.*

The bailiff entered. "All rise, the Honorable Carolyn Ling, presiding."

All rose. Cate wasn't sure her legs would hold her.

"Be seated," the judge requested, and pulled the top file off the stack. "Malloy versus Malloy." She looked up and scanned the room. "Are counsel present?"

"Yes, Your Honor." Both lawyers stood and spoke nearly simultaneously.

"And are your parties present?"

Both attorneys acknowledged that they were.

They remained standing. "Your Honor, counsel for Harve and Helene Malloy and I have agreed that we are close to resolving this case and therefore we request that the court grant us an additional thirty minutes," Grant said.

Helene looked completely shocked, gripping her attorney's arm and whispering loudly.

Cate couldn't make out all the words, but "no" and "impossible" came through clearly. And she pinned her hopes on the fact that Grant said resolved, not negotiating.

"And you agree?" the judge asked the Malloys' counsel.

"Yes, Your Honor."

Judge Ling suddenly looked stern. She scanned each table

and Cate nearly squirmed, feeling as if she were under the microscope.

"I'm going to take the next case," Judge Ling said. "Be prepared to follow, regardless of the timing."

"Thank you, Your Honor," Grant said.

They followed the Malloy cadre out of the courtroom, the door closing behind them just as she heard Judge Ling announce the next case.

Grant pulled them to one end of the corridor. "Gus will explain. I'm sorry I can't right now, I have to use every minute we've got to pull this off. Stay right here, do not engage your in-laws in any conversation."

He met the Malloys' counsel halfway down the corridor. They walked the hall as Grant talked. Cate couldn't hear them at all.

"He's going to present to their counsel the evidence we have," Gus said, filling her in. "Remember, he said he was going to try and get hold of the attorney yesterday after we left you? He was only able to contact the answering service. Today was the first time they had any chance to talk. You know the court uses evidence to rule. We have strong evidence. That's what he's telling him."

Cate watched the two men talk. This was surreal, one moment facing the formality of the court, to this, watching two adversaries conversing in the hallway about the fate of her daughter's future.

The fate of the rest of Cate's life.

The men stopped by a window and continued talking, completely focused on each other.

Something sharp poked into her upper arm. Cate turned to face a furious Helene.

"Haley is a Malloy and by that birthright will be brought up as a Malloy should. Richard had finally come to his senses and was divorcing you, returning to us. Luci would have been the perfect mate for him. She cared that he was heir to our dynasty. She agreed that Haley will be brought up to respect that heritage. Haley is a blood Malloy. You will not have her."

Both attorneys looked in the direction of the raised, hysterical voice. Helene's counsel rushed to her side just as Harve reached her. She screamed at both of them. "Haley is all we have left of Richard, you must see this. This bitch ..." she poked at Cate again, and this time Cate swatted away her finger just as Jason moved in front of her as a shield.

Helene started sobbing loudly. "Haley is all we have of Richard."

Harve gathered his wife close and led her down the hall.

Cate felt arms wrap around her and she was pulled against Jason's chest. She heard the rapid beat of his heart, sure it matched her own.

"Are you okay, did she hurt you?" he asked, pushing her away only long enough to search her face.

"She really does hate me, Jace. And she's so heartbroken that she'd resort to something this heinous." Cate started trembling and allowed Jason to lead her to one of the benches lining the hallway.

Grant approached them. "Time's up. Do you feel like you can do this, Cate? I can proceed without you, but honestly, it'd be far better with you there."

"Of course I'll be there. Do I have a minute?"

"Just about," he answered.

CATE AND GRANT SAT AGAIN AT THE COURTROOM TABLE, WAITING for the Malloys to return.

Judge Ling pulled forward the file just as the door opened

and the Malloys' counsel slipped into his seat. The Malloys were not present.

Cate sent a worried look to Grant.

"Are we ready to proceed?" the judge asked.

Both attorneys stood and agreed. They remained standing. Grant stood completely still, but Cate sensed the tension in his stance.

The judge looked at them and raised a brow.

"Your Honor, we withdraw our petition for custody of Haley Marie Malloy," the Malloys' attorney said.

The air left Cate's lungs.

She desperately needed something to cling to and wished Jason were beside her.

As if reading her thoughts, he reached over the barrier and gripped her shoulder. She covered his hand with hers, trembling and clammy.

"And counsel has agreed?" Judge Ling asked of their side.

"Yes, Your Honor."

"My clients have suggested that Catherine Hemstead Malloy retrieve her daughter immediately."

Cate heard the squeal, not realizing it was her own, until Grant looked down and smiled.

"We agree, Your Honor," he said.

"For the record, the petitioners agreed to withdraw the petition and counsel has agreed for the respondent to pick up Haley Marie Malloy forthwith, and that will be entered as an order of the court," Judge Ling declared.

Cate whirled around and hugged Jason across the railing, tears burning her eyes, rolling down her cheeks. She kissed him, her tears on his lips. "Oh my God, Jace, we won, we actually really won."

"We did, let's go get her."

"Ah, let's get out of here," Grant said.

Cate looked at the judge and would have run up and kissed her too, but knew better. The slight smile on the woman's face told her she understood.

They quickly left the courtroom, and Cate kissed Gus and then Grant and then Jason again, holding onto him tightly.

"What happened to Helene and Harve?" she asked, vowing this was the last time those names would cross her lips.

"You, us, Mark, the truth. When they didn't come in, I thought we might just have nailed it, but had to remember, it's not over until it's over."

The opposing counsel exited the courtroom. "Your daughter is at the Malloys' estate." He shook hands with Grant and left.

Gus immediately called the Watanabe twins, who agreed to meet them at the estate's gate. "Just in case."

15

THE COMPOUND GATES WERE ONCE AGAIN OPEN.

Cate and Jason stood at the front door, Gus and the twins at their back.

Before they could ring the bell, Haley opened the door, squealing, and launched herself at Cate. "Mommy, now we can be together forever. Honest?"

"Honest, little one. Forever." Cate's tears flowed down her cheeks and into Haley's blonde hair.

Jason swallowed hard. This was the reunion that should have happened five days ago. No, this never should have happened in the first place.

He looked up as Emme, the Malloys' housekeeper, brought out two small suitcases and placed them by the front door. He thought he glimpsed a shadow at the window but blinked and it was gone.

He nudged Cate, handing her a bag he'd brought from the car.

She glanced inside and her eyes grew big. "Hey, look what Mr. St. Pierre brought you."

Haley squealed that high-pitched, little-girl squeal as she pulled out Hippity and hugged the bunny fiercely.

"Thank you, Mr. St. Pierre. Can we go now?" Haley asked shyly.

"You bet."

Jason watched as Cate turned her back on the house, her grip on Haley's hand tight.

Then he sensed another person at the door. Gus and the twins shifted their stance and Cate paused, looking back.

"Keep going, Cate, they can't stop you now."

"Will you let us visit her?" Harve called from the doorway.

Cate walked faster. Jason nodded to Gus who, with the twins, flanked her, making sure she was safely out the gate.

Only then did he answer the man. "If I were Cate, I'd tell you to go to hell. But I think you're already there."

Then Jason followed Cate, knowing his help was no longer needed and his job was done.

16

HALEY LOVED THE HALEKULANI. CATE HAD A PRETTY GOOD IDEA that her indulgent attitude had a lot to do with Haley's enthrallment of the hotel. They went swimming in the pool, played in the gentle surf of the sea, built sandcastles and ate shave ice until their tongues turned red and rough from the cherry and pineapple syrup her daughter insisted they both have.

Jason had moved out of the suite shortly after they'd returned to the hotel with Haley.

Cate hadn't seen him all day and felt a heaviness weave through her elation at being reunited with her daughter. He could have stayed and celebrated with them.

Yeah, right. You know it's best this way.

The traumatic day was done. Cate tucked Haley in for the night, then stood watching her sleep, cherishing the delicate crescent of blonde lashes against the tanned baby-soft skin of her cheek. The innocent beauty of her daughter stole her breath, tightened her heart. Cate pulled the light blanket up around Hippity, clasped tightly in Haley's arms, then quietly slipped out the lanai door and looked into the night.

The future she hadn't given much thought to while searching for Haley now loomed starkly in front of her. They needed to leave this improbable haven and head back to Colorado. She'd missed the actual *LA Star* interview Jason had set up and wasn't sure that opportunity was still available. The *About Town* column at the Post was probably gone as well.

She knew, if she were to be honest with herself, that she needed time to adjust to all that happened. The nasty reality was that she really did only have a few thousand dollars as a nest egg.

Haley needed to be talked with as well. To see if the Malloys had inflicted any permanent emotional harm on her daughter. Haley didn't act like it, but Cate was already formulating the gentle probing questions she'd ask in the coming weeks to make sure her daughter didn't have any lasting emotional effects. As far as physical changes, her bangs would grow out quickly.

Cate turned away from the nighttime beauty before her, slipped back inside and snuggled next to Haley in the big bed. She tried to put to rest any more worries about the future. She had Haley back and together they would greet the new day.

IN THE PREDAWN LIGHT, JASON HASTILY SCRIBBLED HIS NOTE, addressed the envelope to Catherine Hemstead, picked up the garment bag and headed out the door.

The crews at the front desk were changing shifts, and with the calm professionalism of the Halekulani staff, assured him they would give Ms. Hemstead the message later in the morning.

"Not too early. Don't wake her," he cautioned. "And please give her this as well," he added, handing them a small black velvet box, then walked out of the hotel.

Even though he'd decided Friday night up on the Pali this

was the best course of action, it had taken him the rest of yesterday to put his plan in action. He'd dragged his heels, an unaccustomed response to a problem that needed solving.

A PremierJet would be available for Cate on Wednesday, giving her more time with Haley to play on the beach. He'd called Dickerson at the *LA Star* and asked if he'd reschedule his interview with Cate. The editor was happy to do so; he still wanted her, so Jason felt sure her immediate job crisis was settled.

Now he headed for the North Shore to learn the game of golf as he'd promised himself while thinking all those hours on Pali. Maybe he'd even take up surfing—he still had the board shorts Gus loaned him.

And he'd start the process of trying to remove Cate from his heart. For six years he'd convinced his brain that he'd fallen out of love with her, that she'd betrayed him, that she wasn't who he thought she was.

But now he had the truth. And granted, it wasn't a pretty picture, as she'd said, but it wasn't all her fault. They'd both destroyed their chance at life together, and also as she'd said, it was too late to go back.

He drove the Mustang across the island. The pink rays of dawn turned the cane and pineapple fields rosy, and pictures of the past days flashed before him as if on a timer: click, click, click. He couldn't shut them off, nor could he stop Cate's voice from playing his mind. Her laughter, her teasing, her cries of passion when they'd made love.

"Damn you, Cate Hemstead. I love you. I. Still. Love. You," he bellowed to nobody but himself.

He pulled sharply onto the side of the road, got out of the car, slammed the door and paced the red dirt, reminding himself of the resolve he made. It wouldn't be easy, but he could go back to his old life. He really had no choice as he reminded himself: they'd both changed, grown into different people, but it was too late.

Jason got back into the car and forced himself to continue his drive away from Cate and Haley, ignoring the voice that told him he was making the second biggest mistake of his life.

THE PREMIERJET IS SCHEDULED FOR WEDNESDAY 6 P.M. YOU'VE GOT Frank and Dani again. The hotel is taken care of. Dickerson still wants you, so call him to set up the interview. Use the check enclosed to give you more breathing room. And Cate, don't be stubborn, enjoy the time with Haley. You both deserve it. As always, Jason.

PS. I couldn't resist. They are you, even if you never wear them.

Cate read the scrawled message twice. The meaning didn't change the second time. Jason had left them. It was truly over. Kaput. Finis.

Broken. Finished.

She crumpled the paper into a tight ball and threw it against the corner. Then, not wanting to lose even this tenuous tie to him, she rushed over and picked up the wad and tried to smooth the wrinkles with her palm, then tucked the note back into the envelope.

Opening the black velvet box, she carefully lifted the golden pearls from their case and held them to her lips. She'd probably never have a place to wear them but knew in her heart of hearts she'd hold them every day and remember this time with Jason, his help, his support and his belief that they would win the fight.

Haley was seated at the small table on the lanai, eating breakfast and watching the big cargo ships head into Honolulu Harbor. Cate breathed rapidly in an effort to stem the hot tears that threatened to fall. She couldn't allow her daughter to see the tears.

"Mommy, can we play on the beach today?"

Cate glanced across the room to see Haley looking uncertainly at her.

"Are you okay, Mommy?"

She swiftly crossed the short distance and kneeled by her daughter. "Of course, little one. You're here, right?"

Perhaps it would be a good idea to be outside and let the novel sights of island life chase away memories. "Are you done with breakfast?" At Haley's nod, Cate held out her hand and relished the warmth of the small one that grasped it. "Then let's go play on the beach."

Foolish woman. Memories of Jason were everywhere. And even if they weren't staring her right in the face, she'd been idiotic to think she wouldn't always carry them in her heart.

Sitting on the warm beach, letting Haley dribble wet sand over her feet, Cate longed to see Jason one last time to thank him for everything he'd done for them.

Haley, tired of playing in the sand, decided to play tag again with the tide. Cate treasured her daughter's high-pitched squeal when the water foamed over and tickled her toes, and wished she could escape her own chaotic thoughts as easily as Haley dodged the tide.

Cate scanned the beach. All the men present paled in comparison to the vibrant, dynamic man named Jason St. Pierre, and she admitted to herself there was an additional trial to go through before she was finished with this part of her life.

For she knew deep in her soul if she didn't ask him if there was any possible chance for them to begin again, to be a family with Haley, she'd always wonder what he would have said.

Believe, Cate, sometimes you just have to believe. Jason's words played in her mind as she called Gus and asked him to find Jason, hoping he was still on the island.

Within the hour, she and Haley were in a rented car and headed to the North Shore.

THE LITANY OF BELIEF FAILED AS CATE DROVE THROUGH THE TWIN lava rock pillars marking the entrance of the resort Jason had chosen. Now about to face him, her qualms far outweighed any belief she might have built up.

A groundskeeper pointed out Jason's bungalow. Cate stopped the car on the crushed shell driveway. Her hands, gripping the steering wheel, turned clammy, and her throat was dry as she tried to swallow around the lump. She couldn't face his rejection. She was about to turn around and drive away when Haley suddenly scrambled out of the car.

"Mr. St. Pierre, look, we're here," she cried as she ran toward him.

There was no turning back.

"And so you are," Jason replied as he scooped up the little girl. What were they doing here? He didn't want them here, not after he'd decided to go on with life as it was before he got in his car and chased Cate down the road.

But Cate was here for a reason, so he'd have to postpone that restart just a bit longer.

"Haley, I just saw a bunch of kids playing tag on the sand. Want to join them?" he asked.

"If you and Mommy come too."

He looked at Cate and saw her nod. "Sure we will."

"Okay."

Jason set her down, took her hand as Cate took the other, and they walked the serpentine path through perfect miniature Japanese gardens to the beach beyond.

Soon Haley was running around, completely at ease with the

other kids. Jason moved a few feet back to the table under a huge banyan tree.

Cate followed.

"This is a surprise."

She wouldn't meet his gaze. "I wanted to thank you, Jason, for everything you did for Haley and me. I couldn't have done this on my own."

He shook his head. "Remember, we had *ho'oponopono.* We were *'ohana.*" He looked at the beach, at Haley and then back at Cate. "You're a smart, resourceful woman. You can accomplish anything you want. Remember that. Remember your spunk, your no-holds-barred attitude. Find it again within yourself and use it."

Jason's words sounded very much like a parting-of-the-ways speech. Cate was sure she imagined the flicker of deep sadness in his eyes before he turned away to watch Haley play with the other kids. Well, now was the time to see if she still had her no-holds-barred attitude. She'd come here with one purpose and would find a way to face whatever came next.

"Jace, Haley's disappearance was the most frightening time of my life. And despite the many times I pushed you to your limits of patience, you still made sure I was included in all this. We've truly been partners in this, and it was that partnership which made it work. I still couldn't have done this without you."

Jason jumped up from the bench as if wanting to flee from her words. Cate wasn't done yet, but she had the feeling of going down for the third time. *You knew that was the risk you'd face when you came out here.*

Despite the midday sun heating her flesh, a chill settled deep in her soul.

Still she plunged on. "Six years ago I screwed up. I didn't know there was infinite room in a heart to hold love. I relied solely on the experience life dealt me before you came into it, and I thought loving you was all I could handle. I was so terribly wrong.

"I love you. I always have. I came today because I wanted to ask you if there is a chance to start again, to be a family. I know it's a lot to forgive, and I understand if you can't," she finished softly.

He flinched.

She had her answer.

Cate gathered her satchel and called to Haley, who came running with a shell in her hand. "Come on, little one, time for us to go home."

"Here, Mr. St. Pierre, you can have this," Haley put the shell on the picnic table, and Cate's heart broke. She needed to get out of there, now. She grabbed her daughter's hand, and they headed back on the same serpentine path they'd walked before.

Haley turned around and waved to Jason. "Bye."

Cate turned back as well, and her heart caught at the air of loneliness that surrounded him. This last image would be burned into her mind forever.

Haley stopped by the koi pond they'd passed on their way to the beach, intrigued by the groundskeeper feeding the huge tangerine-colored fish. The man gave her some of the pellets and showed her how to feed them. Cate itched to get away and experienced a sudden sense of déjà vu when she couldn't wait to leave Highgate and Haley hadn't wanted to.

She and Haley were once again on their own, about to start a new life. This time, Cate might be facing the future with a solid job, but still without the man she knew would have made her complete. She'd had a fleeting taste of heaven, and now had to get used to being alone.

Haley begged to stay and feed the fish. Another few minutes wouldn't hurt, right?

Wrong.

Being anywhere in the vicinity of Jason hurt like hell.

CATE'S WORDS HUNG IN THE AIR.

Could he forgive her? Hadn't he already, from the moment he'd heard the truth, and realized his part in pushing them apart? Hadn't he yelled to the sky that he still loved her?

How could he have asked her to keep believing through all this and now not take that leap of faith himself?

They had a past. It was now a part of who they were, but did that mean they couldn't have a future?

He watched her leave. With each step she took, his spirit deflated. Then Haley turned around to yell goodbye, and he straightened from pride, becoming almost rigid when her mother turned around too. The distance was too far to see what emotion her eyes held, but her body sagged, and he could almost feel the weight of what it cost her to come to him. Then mother and daughter turned back and continued walking away.

Without analyzing his decision to death and losing the second chance of a lifetime, Jason headed down the same path Cate and Haley had taken.

When he didn't see them, fear moved his feet, and he broke into a run.

By the koi pond, he spied Haley feeding the fish and Cate sitting on a bench nearby watching her.

"Cate!"

She slowly turned at the sound of his voice and stood, her legs rubbery. Her heart raced, her stomach danced, and she had the oddest sense of a girl being out on her first date. Jason's whiskey brown eyes were dark with emotion, but his face gave no indication as to which emotion.

"You asked if we could be a family, and could we put the past behind us, could we start again. Could I forgive you?"

She looked down, concentrating on the coarse grass beside the path, suddenly afraid that he was completely severing their last ties.

Strong fingers nudged her chin upward. Still she refused to look at him.

"Look at me."

A deep sigh escaped her soul as she gathered courage and looked up.

"Can you forgive me?"

She swallowed hard. "Jace, I'm the one who screwed up—"

"No, you said it, we've both changed. The past is a lesson, the future is to be embraced, and frankly I don't want it to stretch out in front of me, empty of you, guessing what might have been."

"But I—"

"You had a beautiful child, and while the circumstances might not have been ideal for parents, the love she's known from you and from Richard will carry her forward. You never had that as a child, and for me, while my aunt tried, she didn't know how to show affection to a child. It's time to change that."

He cupped her face; his thumbs caressed her jaw line. Brown eyes melded with green. "I love you, my Cate. I've always loved you," he vowed, his voice husky as he drew her face closer and covered her lips in a healing kiss.

She lifted her mouth just a fraction from his. "I know—"

"That we have a whole lifetime of new memories ahead of us?" he whispered.

Her knees trembled with the power of his words, and she realized everything that needed to be said had been, and it was now time to move forward.

"Yes." She tunneled her hands through his sable hair,

bringing his head closer and deepened their kiss. Making promises of her own.

"I love you," she whispered, breaking their kiss just long enough to say the words again.

"Aloha, my Cate," he said, and she knew with all her heart, this time it meant love, not something else.

At the high squeal of childish laughter, Jason broke their kiss as he raised his head to see what caused Haley's burst of laughter.

Cate turned in his arms in time to see Haley holding up a nibble of food and the large koi squirming on top of one another to reach it. Haley clapped her hands delightedly when one koi reached up the farthest to snatch the nibble.

Jason rested his chin against Cate's shining crown of hair. He wrapped his arms around her, holding her close to his heart. "Haley is with her mommy, her mommy is with me, and someday, if Haley wishes, I'll adopt her. We're *'ohana*."

They knew believing is more than halfway to achieving your dream.

~ THE END ~

Thank you (Mahalo) for reading *Dare To Believe*. I truly hope you enjoyed. If so, I'd deeply appreciate your review. Our success in this incredibly competitive world relies on, yep, reviews. Again, thank you.

And find the first chapter of Brushed By Betrayal ~ Book 2 in the Kahuna Series at the end of this book. I hope you enjoy.

LETTER TO MY READERS

I'm often asked how I find stories to write. My answer may sound simplistic, but it's true, I get inspiration from life, news, conversations. And sometimes from traveling. I had planned on living in Hawaii, attending grad school at U of H Manoa Campus. In fact, I'd moved there. But a variety of things happened and I moved back to the mainland. Sounds like another story, right?

But Hawaii has always stayed with me from the first trip there I took with my father. There is a mystical and practical side to the islands that I love.

The places in the book are all places I've been to and loved. Some are gone now, as progress takes over and land is sold.

I hope to return to the islands more often. My husband and I honeymooned there, while our luggage went on to China, was hit on the tarmac by a baggage cart and returned to us in pieces. We shopped for clothes at the International Market Place, now gone. We ate on the beach, we drove around the islands.

It's time to return, they are calling to us. And I want to write Book Three in the Kahuna Group, which means I have research to do.

I have a newsletter that I enjoy writing and sending monthly. Keeping you up to date on my writing, my crazy busy life and often my photography. And don't forget I love hearing from you!

ALSO BY L.A. SARTOR

TO FIND ALL MY BOOKS

Amazon Author Page

STAR LIGHT ~ STAR BRIGHT

A Romantic Christmas Series Set In Snowy Boulder, Colorado

Be Mine This Christmas Night

Forever Yours This New Year's Night

Believe In Me This Christmas Morn

Dream Of Me This Christmas Eve

THE CARSWELL ADVENTURE SERIES

Heart Pounding Adventure With A Dash of Romance Set In Exotic Locales

Stone Of Heaven

Viking Gold

THE KAHUNA GROUP SERIES

Suspense With A Dash of Romance

Dare To Believe

Brushed By Betrayal

THE PLANTATION SERIES

Pure Romance Set in Costa Rica On A Rare Cacao Plantation

Prince Of Granola

THE JENNA HART JEWELRY MYSTERIES

A Cozy Mystery Series Set in the Colorado Ski Town Of Angelcroft

Tick Tock Dead

Capture the code with a mobile device's QR reader to see all of
L.A. Sartor's Books

ACKNOWLEDGMENTS

Audra Harders, an extraordinary author who has been beside me on this journey since we both started. Well, almost. I did start a month before her. Audra, I know I couldn't have done this without you.

Visit http://www.audraharders.com and see what she's up to.

Theresa Rizzo, who created writing retreats where we could bury ourselves in our work, and who listened to me when I was certain I'd never make this a reality, then told me I would. Thank you.

My Editor, Ellis Vidler, who has a passion for helping make books the best they can be. Thank you.

ABOUT THE AUTHOR

I started writing as a child, really. A few things happened on the way to becoming a published author ... specifically, a junior high school teacher who told me I couldn't write because I didn't want to study grammar.

That English teacher stopped my writing for years. But the muse couldn't be denied, and eventually I wrote, a lot, some of it award winning.

My husband told me repeatedly that independent publishing was becoming a valid way to publish a novel. I didn't believe him. I thought indie meant vanity press.

I couldn't have been more wrong.

I started pursuing this direction seriously, hit the keyboard, learned a litany of new things and published my first novel. My second book became a bestseller, and I'm absolutely on the right course in my life.

I live in Colorado with my husband Gary whom I met on a blind date—I can't imagine life without my best friend. We play in the mountains and travel as much as possible.

Find me at www.lesliesartor.com

BRUSHED BY BETRAYAL

BOOK 2 IN THE KAHUNA GROUP SERIES

CHAPTER ONE

THE WOMAN WHINED IN JADE LAURENT'S EAR. "YOU PROMISED ME the sapphire would be delivered today. The bank is going to close in an hour. Why can't you stand by your promises? Your father always did—"

"Evan has the Khan, Mrs. Cole. He's just been delayed." Jade counted to three, then four, frustrated by not only the haughty English accent Mrs. Elvina Cole layered on like treacle but by her phone calls every thirty minutes since noon—more annoying as Jade had already told her that Evan's flight hadn't been scheduled to arrive until 2 p.m. "I can't control traffic. I'm sure—"

"Don't interrupt me. I used to be treated like I was the most important client Laurent Art Brokers had. Now I don't even get a courtesy call or a car to pick me up and take me to the office. It's a ride-share or, heaven forbid, an American taxi."

True, Jade admitted to herself. Things had changed after her father died. She brushed aside the guilt Mrs. C was so good at inserting slyly into any conversation and focused on the real problem. It was just shy of four o'clock, and Evan should have been here by now. It was only an hour's drive from Denver International Airport.

It had been planned so that he had enough time to get to the office and have Mrs. Cole watch as Jade tested and inspected the famous and supposedly cursed sapphire. Then they'd have plenty of time to get Mrs. Cole to the bank. But traffic between DIA and Boulder was never predictable.

The haughty voice continued. "I don't know why you had Evan Fischer courier the Khan. I thought you were going to Singapore to handle it."

"Because this is what he does. He's a master at it. Dad trusted him implicitly, and Evan has done this for decades. It was stated in our contract, remember?"

"Hmph. So you say. I want you or Evan to drive me to the bank. That, too, was in our contract."

"Naturally. In fact, if this works for you, since time is short, we'll come to your house for the delivery and testing. Then we can take you immediately to the bank. I'll pack my equipment as soon as we hang up."

"And then you'll wait until I'm done to bring me home. Yes, I'll accept that. You call the minute you're on your way."

Jade looked to the ceiling as if the cream-colored plaster could offer her a snappy comeback. "Yes, of course," was all she managed, only to realize the line was dead. "Damn."

The door to her office opened and her best friend, Megan Rice, the woman who kept everything straight at Laurent Art Brokers, poked her head in. "Am I safe to enter? I saw the phone light go off, and knowing who you were talking to, I'm just being cautious in case you were going to throw the phone at the door."

Megan stepped into the office holding a crystal diffuser of her favorite lavender oil and put it on Jade's side of the partners' desk. "Too bad Mrs. Cole has the direct office line, so I can't stall her for you."

"Yeah, one of Dad's white-glove treatments for special clients." Jade air-quoted *special*. "How Dad stood her all those years is a mystery. And thank goodness she doesn't have my cell number. That was an excellent suggestion on your part."

Megan curtsied, holding out her forest green tunic with one hand, the other tucked behind her as if she were on stage.

Jade's buddy was taller than her own five-two by a few inches, but Megan still could be mistaken for a pixie, with her tumbled mass of fiery red curls and laughing blue eyes.

Holding up a finger to her lips, Jade feigned deep thought. "I wonder if we could fake a busy signal just for that line?"

"Greg would know how. I'll ask him when he gets back."

Jade knew better than to ask where Megan's fiancé, Greg Harrison, was now. The only thing Megan would be able to say is "on a stakeout." She never knew where or for how long. Meg had the tolerance level of a saint, but Jade could see past the mask of bravery and forbearance and knew her buddy was always worried when her fiancé was away. "Greg's a genius, so I have no doubt he could rig something like that. But seriously, the woman is a complete piece of work. I wonder if she's always been like that? I know her son loves her, but even he told me he can't tolerate her for long. I wish he were here now."

"Yes, she dotes on him. Too bad David Cole, son extraordinaire to quote his mum, lives in Hawaii. I'm sure he chose that spot for his tech biz on purpose. He can still live in the US yet be as far away as possible from 'Mother.'"

Jade nodded, completely agreeing with Megan. David was the antithesis of his prim and proper mother. She pictured him —dark blond hair on the longish side, serious blue eyes that could twinkle with a joke—and realized it was only late morning in Hawaii. When he was in town, they often got together and once had compared notes on what their typical day was like. She knew he'd already been out for a ride on the waves with his traditional longboard and would have finished his jog around his upscale Black Point neighborhood. By now David would be at work in a downtown Honolulu high rise that housed his booming tech biz. He'd gone from a simple laptop to a billion-dollar company with offices in four global centers of commerce, and he'd offered to show her any of the cities firsthand. Maybe that was exactly what she needed—a long vacation on the beach instead of sitting here, fending off an impatient client.

Megan pointed to the crystal diffuser she'd brought in. "Breathe. Now."

Holding the small container to her nose, Jade inhaled the calming scent deeply. "If this weren't the biggest commission I've done to date, I wouldn't have taken it, but the acquisition of the Khan will be, forgive me, the crown jewel of my tenure as head of Laurent Art Brokers."

Megan nodded, then looked like she wanted to say something about what this day honestly meant. Instead, she pirouetted and headed back to her domain, the main room of the business, closing the door softly behind her.

Grateful for Megan's reticence, Jade rubbed her temples. She wasn't particularly worried about Evan's late arrival, though an update text would have helped her cause with Mrs. Elvina Cole. And with such a beautiful early spring day she was sure the roads were filled with traffic. Still, he should have let her know he was delayed.

Letting loose a deep, from-the-heart sigh, Jade looked across the partners' desk to the vacant space. Nothing, not the biggest commission to date, not the amazing weather, not Evan's delayed arrival, could camouflage what this day really represented.

It was the one-year anniversary of her father's untimely death.

He died by a hit and run in the very parking lot of the building they owned, located near Boulder's Pearl Street Mall. His case was still open, but she knew it would now be nearly impossible for the perpetrator to be found and serve the sentence for his or her crime.

Getting up, she moved to her father's side of the desk and sat in his antique chair, hearing its springs creak. She picked up his pipe and inhaled the sweet scent still lingering in the burled wooden bowl, though it was growing fainter by the day.

Gerard Laurent's Hermès tweed jacket still hung on the Arts and Craft oak coat rack. The two comfortable leather chairs for clients, grouped with an old steamer trunk fashioned into a table, stood as vacant sentinels to his absence.

The emptiness of the inner sanctum, as her father called it, exacerbated the increasing discomfort she experienced over running the business alone. She hadn't taken the time to examine the root of the irritant. It wasn't running the business. She could handle it and its often demanding clients, even if she didn't like that schmoozing part of the business.

Maybe she was simply tired of the loneliness.

Jade picked at the dent her father had made in the cherry desk during a rare fit of anger, something she'd witnessed only once. She'd just entered their office and he was on the phone, gesturing wildly with his heavy antique brass paper opener. Then he slammed it on the desk, scattering the thick sheets of luxurious writing paper. Abruptly ending the call, he gathered the papers and stuffed them into his coat pocket. At her questioning look, he told her he'd be back later and left.

He was, but the next day security cameras were installed in the office and hall, alarms in both her and her father's home, and new security protocols for the building itself. Swipe cards for after hours and weekends and a camera in the elevator. It all seemed excessive to Jade, but no matter how much she pressed her father, he remained mute. As did their colleague, Evan Fischer.

Which brought her thoughts full circle.

She realized a huge amount of the frustration she was feeling with Mrs. Cole was really a reaction to the sad date. Jade had dreaded this day, knowing the wounds that were just beginning to scab were going to be torn open and tears would fall again.

The phone on her desk shrilled again and she simply ignored it.

How did you handle them, Dad? It isn't easy dealing with prima donna clients, yet you always smiled and charmed them.

Suddenly the tears fell hot and fast. Not moving or bothering to wipe them away, she let them fall, trying to breathe through the incredible pain of loss.

The door to her office opened again. In a flash she was out of her chair and wrapped in the arms of Megan.

She had no idea how long she stood there cocooned in the warm support of her best friend. The only sounds were of her own ragged pain. But slowly the tears stopped, and her breath came easier.

Jade stepped back and Megan pulled a tissue from her pocket, offering it to her. "Listen, I know you said you wanted to be alone tonight, but how about you come out to dinner with Malcolm and me? He's finishing up a case and we're celebrating."

Malcolm Talbot, the co-owner of Harrison & Talbot Investigations, was the only source of news about Megan's fiancé, Greg, who was on some stealthy, no personal contact job —somewhere.

Jade pegged Malcolm as the kind of guy who wouldn't appreciate having to cheer up a morose woman. She knew Megan adored him as a friend, but Malcolm's choice of women leaned toward the witty, stylish, and magazine cover-worthy. The exact opposite of Jade Laurent. Not that she wasn't stylish—she loved clothes, but she wasn't witty and certainly not cover-worthy.

She took the tissue Megan offered, wiped her face, then shook her head. "Thanks for the offer, but no. I'm betting that you want to pump Malcolm for information about Greg."

"There's nothing he'll tell me that you can't hear. So that excuse won't wash," Megan said, her arms now crossed.

Jade gave Megan a weak grin over her militant stance. "No, you two go, celebrate, get news on Greg. But I do think I'll head home if you can hold down the fort. I'll text Evan to come to the house, and we'll immediately head off to Mrs. C's. It's really as quick to get there from my home as it is from here."

Just then, the ring of bells indicated someone had entered the office.

"Evan," they exclaimed in unison and hurried to greet him.

Instead they found Smythe, an unremarkable man except for his talent at reproducing artists' work. He studied two periods intensely, allowing him to reproduce those works with impeccable detail. American Modernism with Georgia O'Keefe was his favorite artist and the Impressionist period with Mary Cassatt his top choice.

"Great, you're both here. I can't wait to show you how my latest commission turned out."

Jade bit back her groan and Megan plastered on a look of interest. Only Jade knew it was totally feigned.

Laurent Art Brokers had increasing numbers of wealthy clients across the world who paid top dollar for reproductions of their priceless original art to hang in their homes or offices while keeping their originals in a home or off-premises vault. In fact, the practice of hanging reproductions was becoming more common even for museum collections as thieves were becoming cleverer and artwork priceless.

Smythe, who had no first name they knew of, was as usual hunched over. Megan thought he seemed to have some sort of posture issue. His ratty, faded baseball cap was apparently a permanent feature, probably to cover his balding pate, even though he had a gray scraggly ponytail sticking out the back. And his eyes were magnified by thick glasses. In fact, he looked a bit like a hunched over old frog.

Yet he moved quickly, almost darting to the door as he hauled the large canvas backward, so the stretchers showed, as always refusing any help. "Ready?"

Jade's interest was real even though his timing was bad. After all, detecting forgeries was part of her specialty, and she loved the challenge—far more interesting than negotiating deals and soothing difficult customers.

The quality of Smythe's work had never let her down. He truly was one of the best reproduction artists in the world.

With a flourish, he whirled the painting around. It was a stunning reproduction of Georgia O'Keeffe's *Mariposa Lilies and Indian Paintbrush*, painted in 1941.

"May I?" Jade asked the man.

"I expect you to. It's your reputation on the line as well as mine."

But today it took more than a little effort for her to switch on her art-expertise mode. She carefully scanned the painting, noting that the strokes were perfect, the signature flawless. Then, looking at the back, she noted that even the wood stretchers holding the canvas were of the era's style and right age. Smythe was a perfectionist, and all the details mattered to him. A client or his "audience" wouldn't be able to tell whether the stretchers or the paint era were correct. All that mattered was that the client could show off their painting, confident in the knowledge their original was safe and secure.

Jade nodded. "Fine work. The clients will be incredibly happy. It would take a much closer examination, even infrared reflectography or mass spectrometry equipment, to detect this as a reproduction."

Smythe beamed. "I'll get it crated tonight and hopefully freighted tomorrow."

He carried out the painting, and Megan closed the door behind him. "Such a strange dude."

Jade nodded. "Another holdover from Dad."

And with that, her stomach roiled and her head swam. She extended her hand to steady herself, finding nothing to hold onto until Megan grabbed her.

"Listen, go home. Eat. I know you haven't had anything all day. Anyway, there is no way now that you'll make the bank in—"

As if on cue, the phone in Jade's office rang again. It could only be Mrs. Cole.

Jade shook her head at Megan's raised brow. "To be honest Meg, I don't know what to think about Evan. He always stays in touch and I have no news to tell Mrs. Cole."

The phone continued its shrill tone. Jade snatched up the receiver on Megan's desk and pushed the button for her private line. "Mrs. Cole, I haven't heard more from Evan, and we won't make it to the bank in time now. So I'm suggesting we meet early, here at the office just before the banks open. I'll send a car for you."

"You are an incredible disappointment to me, Jade Laurent."

"I'm sure I am, but there is nothing more I can do at the moment." And with that she replaced the receiver in its cradle.

"Go. I've got the office, and it's near closing time anyway," Megan said.

Jade didn't need another nudge. Bolting into her office, she gathered her phone, purse, and jacket, still fighting the queasiness roiling her stomach. She lifted a hand to Megan as she dashed through the reception area and left the suite. For a nanosecond she deliberated taking the elevator. Not relishing the stale air of the enclosure even for a brief time, she beat back the nausea and ran down the oak stairs of the two-story office building her father had built and she now owned.

The chill in the spring air did little to calm her stomach as she drove the short distance from downtown Boulder to Mapleton Hill and home.

THIS LAST CASE TOOK MORE OUT OF MALCOLM THAN HE'D thought possible. He was barely forty, yet right now he felt several decades older as he climbed the stairs to Laurent Art Brokers to pick up Megan for dinner.

Not only had his client withheld vital information, he'd lied. Perhaps the better description was *overstated his position.* Eventually, it came down to having a bit more than a heart-to-heart talk with the man, getting to the real issue and not just the grievance. It was done, the client happy, and the swindler facing a long string of indictments.

Malcolm shook off his feeling of dullness and stopped at the brass plaque denoting Megan's workplace. As per long-standing habit, he quickly surveyed the area. A discrete camera focused on the door and would show any visitor. A small buzzer was set into the framework. There was also a heavy brass knob, which he tried.

Locked.

He glanced at his watch, realizing it was a bit after five o'clock. He knew Megan was in. They'd texted not ten minutes ago. Pressing the buzzer, he smiled up at the camera. When the snick of locks opening sounded, he turned the knob and entered.

Megan held up one finger as she talked on the phone—more like grimacing than smiling, he noted, as he could hear a woman talking in loud emphatic tones with an English accent. While he waited, he took the time to glance around the large room and admired how it was cleverly divided into Megan's workspace and a foyer-sitting area, complete with coffee bar in a simple yet classic pecan armoire. Probably an antique, and he'd bet anything those were china cups for the clients. Various types of artwork graced the walls, but he didn't know a Picasso from a Renoir. No couches, but several armchairs that had high backs. Queen Anne, he thought he remembered hearing when he was touring a mansion at a charity gig.

His gaze moved to Megan's area of the office. Yep, it was all hers. A plank of stained teak atop black metal legs, a large laptop, phone, a tall stack of files, and the always-filled cup of coffee within easy reach.

Finally, she hung up the phone. "You look awful."

He grinned. Only Megan and Greg, his partner, would dare be that honest with him. "And you look a bit harried."

"It's been more than a trying day." She got up from behind her desk and he met her halfway, enfolding her in a hug. Three years ago, they'd briefly dated. Megan hadn't observed his unspoken rules regarding the way he conducted relationships. She'd call him for a picnic or a drive in the mountains and surprisingly he'd go with her. She frequently refused his invitations if they involved going to the latest opening or gala.

Megan listened instead of talked and soon he'd opened up to her as he'd never done with a woman before. They became friends instead of lovers. Then he introduced her to his partner, Greg Harrison.

Shortly, Malcolm was going to be best man at their July wedding.

Now, as he smiled in sympathy, she pointed at the phone and rolled her eyes. "That was a client who has been a pain in the patootie from day one. Long before Jade was the remaining Laurent of Laurent Art Brokers. And worse, today is the anniversary of Jade's father's accident."

Malcolm had heard all about that hit and run and done some digging on his own, but the trail went cold almost immediately. And he knew all too well how these sad anniversaries seemed to take one by surprise and bring up all sorts of memories. Eventually one could remember with less intensity. But he knew from experience that to reach that point usually took longer than 365 days. "Do you want to call off our dinner and be with Jade?"

"Thanks for offering. I already suggested she have dinner with us, knowing you wouldn't really mind. But she refused. So let's go out, you can tell me about Greg, and we can share an expensive bottle of wine, your treat. Then once I have you mellowed out, you'll feel like telling me if you're ready to cut back a bit."

"The wine sounds great, as does a dinner with my favorite girl, but I can answer your question right now. Yes, I need a break of some sort. With no vacations, no breaks in case load for the past fifteen years, I think I need a change of scenery. Once you and Greg get back from your honeymoon, I'll figure it out."

"Finally. Let's start figuring it out tonight. Just let me finish making a note in Mrs. Cole's file and put everything away."

A singsong note chimed from her computer. Returning to her desk she glanced at the camera view of the door. "Hmmm, I don't recognize them. Let's wait until they leave, and then you can buy that really great bottle of Cabernet, okay?"

MEGAN'S WORDS IMMEDIATELY DROVE HIM TO LOOK AT HER computer screen. Malcolm was overly cautious, to the point of annoyance according to Megan, but it didn't matter. It's what he did.

He recognized the two men on the monitor and their presence never signified good news. "That's odd."

They stood at the office door, looking up at the camera as he had minutes ago. As usual, Tomba was rocking on his heels.

"Malcolm?"

"Meg, I know them. They're police detectives. There is no reason why these guys should show up here unless it's something new about Gerard's death. Maybe they found a lead. You should let them in."

As Megan scanned his face with a question on hers, he simply nodded, hiding his unease. This was Denver PD at the door, not Boulder PD who should be handling the case.

She pressed the button to unlock the door, and the two men in street clothes with jackets likely concealing their weapons entered the office. Then they stopped in their tracks.

"Talbot, what are you doing here?"

"Why is Denver Homicide here?" Malcolm countered.

"Denver Homicide?" Megan echoed.

"We need to talk to a Jade Laurent. There is no home address for her, or phone number. We got this address off—"

He shut up as if saying too much.

"She's home." Megan's voice quivered just a bit.

"It's vital we talk with her tonight," the heavier of the two said. "Who are you?" he asked, looking at Megan.

Malcolm shook his head in mock dismay. "Meg, these guys, who really are nicer than they're behaving, are Tomba, the one who asked the question, and Moore, the nicer one. Don't let them scare you."

"Megan Rice, assistant to Jade Laurent *and* her best friend. Is this about her father's death?"

"No, ma'am."

"Ah, see, you got a 'ma'am.'" Malcolm tried to lighten the atmosphere.

"She'll be here in the morning," Megan offered.

"This really can't wait until then."

Malcolm met Meg's glance, which told him that she wanted to be around if Tomba and Moore were going to Jade's house. And whatever the issue was sounded serious enough that they needed to go tonight. "We'll meet you there. Do not go to the door until we're with you, as a courtesy to me."

Moore nodded. "We owe you that."

Only then did Megan write Jade's address on a piece of paper and hand it to Moore.

FINALLY JADE HEARD THE SHORT RIFT OF CAROLE KING ON HER phone. Evan was at the door. She didn't try and hide the tear tracks on her cheeks. Evan would understand better than anyone. In fact, she needed to see him, to share this moment with him. She knew he missed Gerard Laurent as much as she did.

Untangling from the afghan she'd wrapped around herself, she jumped off the couch and swiftly opened the door, only remembering at the last moment she was supposed to check the camera monitor on her phone. A lesson her dad tried to instill, but one that apparently never took hold.

Instead of Evan, an anxious Megan and an unsmiling Malcolm stood there along with two unfriendly-looking men behind them. Scanning her buddy's anxious face, Jade's stomach dropped. "Meg, what's wrong? Oh my God, is it Greg? Is he okay?" She clutched her friend's arm.

"No, it's not Greg—"

"May we come in?" Malcolm asked.

Jade glanced at him, then back at Megan, who nodded. She didn't believe Malcolm would bring anyone to her home who wasn't vetted by him, but who were those men and why was Megan involved?

The man next to Megan answered her unspoken question. "Detectives Tomba and"—he nodded toward the second man— "Moore." Jade's heart skipped a beat. Police? She opened the door wide to let them in, trying to slow the sudden acceleration in her breathing. Leading the way into her dimly lit living room, she turned on a few lamps as she passed.

Once all five of them crowded inside the small room, it felt claustrophobic, so she moved to stand in front of the fireplace. She glanced at the couch, realizing her afghan was bunched up, taking up most of the room on the Ultrasuede cushions. Crossing to the couch, she picked up the still-warm throw and methodically folded it, then tucked it inside the ottoman, a gesture she made only to calm herself. The wine bottle and glass could stay right where they were, but now people could sit.

Nobody did. They were apparently waiting until she stopped fluttering around.

Taking several slow, deep breaths, hoping they might soothe her, also failed. She hid her shaking hands in the pockets of the fleece tunic she wore. This visit was reminiscent of the police coming to tell her of her father's "accident." In fact, that was probably the very reason they were here, to shed new light on the investigation. Finally.

But then why were Megan and Malcolm also here?

The ticking of the clock on the mantel behind her seemed to pound its rhythm into her ears.

"You are Jade Laurent?"

"I am, and you are?" She couldn't recall either of their names.

"Detective Tomba from Denver Homicide." He repeated his name as he pulled a leather case out of his jacket pocket and flipped it open to reveal his shield.

She didn't glance at it, knowing since Malcolm was here, they were who they said. "Denver? Have you found a new lead in my father's accident?"

"No, ma'am. Detective Moore." The smaller man introduced himself and did the same routine with his shield. He then removed a small folio from his upper pocket and withdrew a glassine envelope, handing it to her. "Does this belong to you?"

Fighting the disappointment that these men offered her nothing more on her father's investigation, it took her a moment to register that the envelope held a Laurent Art Broker's business card. "It's a card for my business."

Megan moved to stand beside her and, as Jade scanned her buddy's face, she saw her friend nod toward Malcolm. Jade got the message that she wasn't alone in whatever this was about. Their support gave her a small measure of courage.

"Do you usually have business cards without names on them?" The bigger detective asked.

That was an odd question. "Yes, I have my cards. Meg," she nodded toward her friend, "has cards with her name on them. And we have blank cards. It's standard procedure in our business."

"Can you recognize the writing on the back?" Detective Moore asked.

Jade turned over the envelope to read aloud, "Please let Jade Laurent know she's next and the clock has ticked down to now.

Then the circle will be complete." The black writing slashed across the card's cream-colored surface was in stark contrast with the polite wording of the message.

Megan's gasp mirrored her own shock.

Jade thrust the card back at the detective as Malcolm moved forward with hand outstretched for it.

"Denver Homicide? Where did you find that?" She pointed to the packet Malcolm now held.

"At the scene of a death."

Evan? No, no! But who else could it be? Jade's knees buckled and had Malcolm not moved quickly and grasped her elbow, she'd have fallen to the floor. He manhandled her to the couch, and she barely made it as blackness narrowed her vision.

"Keep your head down," Malcolm directed as he pressed her shoulders forward. "Meg, water?"

Moments later, a finger raised her chin and an opened bottle of water was put to her lips.

"Can you drink some?"

Jade managed a small sip.

"Another," he ordered.

She did as commanded, then tried to form words. "Where?"

"Late this afternoon, a gentleman was found in the restroom of Denver International Airport. This was near the body, er, person."

"Did you ID the ..."

"No ma'am. There was no identification on him."

It couldn't be Evan. Impossible.

But he hasn't called or texted since the plane touched down. That's so unlike him. He'd know I would worry.

"Was there a prosthesis for his right arm?"

"We're not allowed to touch the body to check other than to see if the victim is alive. The coroner will have that information."

A tiny flame of hope ignited deep inside her.

"Ma'am, your business card was on the floor, next to the body. We need a positive ID."

"Tomba, can't this wait until morning?" Malcolm asked in sharp tones.

"No, Talbot, it can't. The coroner has requested that a forensic pathologist conduct an autopsy. It was an unattended death, and then there was that note on the back of the business card."

Then the words in the message hit her. The card said *next*. Was it a threat? Was *she* next?

Dimly through the haze of fear of what she'd find at the coroner's office and the note's threat, she felt the warmth of Malcom's hand on her shoulder, offering support.

The thinner detective kneeled by Jade. "We need you to come with us to the Denver medical examiner's office—tonight."

A sob came from Megan's direction. She looked to find her friend's fist pressed against her lips, trying to hold back her emotion.

Jade reached out a shaking hand to her, and Meg moved over to grasp it, her hand as icy as her own. "It's possible it's not Evan, Meg. It's still possible."

"You're not going alone, Jade. I'm coming too." Meg sniffled.

"I'll bring them both," Malcolm offered.

Amazon